DOG

DOG

Daniel Pennac

translated by Sarah Adams

CANDLEWICK PRESS
CAMBRIDGE, MASSACHUSETTS

Originally published by Éditions Nathan, Paris, France,
in the *Arc en Poche* series

Text copyright © 1982, 1994 by Éditions Nathan, Paris, France, and
copyright © 2001 by Nathan / VUEF, Paris, France
This edition copyright © 2002 by Daniel Pennac
Illustrations copyright © 2002 by Britta Teckentrup

English translation by Sarah Adams

First U.S. edition 2004

Library of Congress Cataloging-in-Publication Data
Pennac, Daniel.
[Cabot-Caboche. English]
Dog / Daniel Pennac ; translated by Sarah Adams — 1st U.S. ed.
p. cm.
Summary: Rescued from certain death by a kindly dog at the city dump,
an abandoned puppy grows up fending for himself until he finds a home
with a willful little girl. Could she be the mistress of his dreams?
ISBN 0-7636-2421-7
1. Dogs — Juvenile fiction. [1. Dogs — Fiction.] I. Adams, Sarah, date.
II. Title.
PZ10.3.P29955Do 2004
[Fic] — dc22   2003055335

10 9 8 7 6 5 4 3 2 1

Printed in the United States of America

This book was typeset in Centaur MT.

Candlewick Press
2067 Massachusetts Avenue
Cambridge, Massachusetts 02140

visit us at www.candlewick.com

Contents

Cold Dinner

"*Who do you think you are?*"

Mrs. Squeak is squeaking. She has a piercing voice. Her words bounce off the kitchen walls, the ceiling, and the floor. Her squeaks get mixed up with the clatter of dishes. There's so much noise, the words have stopped making sense. Dog flattens his ears and waits for things to calm down. He's heard it all before anyway. So what if they rescued him? So what if he used to be homeless? He's got nothing to hide.

Ouch! There she goes again. Why does Mrs. Squeak always squeak? And why does she carry on that way? If Dog didn't need four legs to stand on, he'd block his ears with his front paws. But he doesn't like copying human beings.

"Aren't you going to eat your dinner?"

No, he's not going to eat his dinner. Dog's rolled himself up into a ball of fur in front of his plate. His mouth and ears have disappeared.

"Fine. Have it your own way. But I'm warning you," squeaks Mrs. Squeak, "that's all you're getting."

The door opens and Mr. Muscle's huge shoes come right up to Dog's nose.

"What's all the shouting about?" His voice rumbles out of his vast body. The words roll around the kitchen like rocks in an avalanche or (since Dog has never seen an avalanche) like the creaky old bedsteads, television carcasses, and broken fridges that came crashing down in the dump outside the town where Dog used to live. Dog doesn't have happy memories of the dump. But more about that later.

"It's Dog. He won't eat his dinner."

"Why make such a fuss? Just shut him in the kitchen. He'll eat it in the end."

Those gigantic feet swivel around, and Mr. Muscle grumbles as he goes out. "Gets on my nerves, that mutt. . . ."

Mutt is another word for dog. There are plenty more names like that, and none of them are very polite. Cur, mongrel, hound, pooch — Dog knows them all, and he gave up being offended by them long ago.

"Did you hear that? In the kitchen. All night. And you'll stay there till you've eaten your dinner!"

She's got nerve. As if Dog's ever been allowed to sleep anywhere but the kitchen. As if they'd let him spend the night on the soft, fleecy living-room carpet, or in the hall armchair with its smell of old leather, or on Plum's bed . . .

He knows the ice-cold kitchen tiles back to front, thank you. Nothing new there. Tip-tap, tip-tap. Mrs. Squeak trips out of the room on heels as high and pointy as her words, and the door closes with a bang. Silence. The long silence of the night.

3

Something Funny's Going On

It's not that Dog's lost his appetite. No, it's not that. And the dinner isn't bad either. No worse than any other dinner. If you sniff hard enough, it even gives off a whiff of meat, though only very faintly.

No, Dog's not eating his dinner because he's in a mood. He's in a mood because Plum's in a mood. And when Plum's in a mood, she doesn't eat. So he doesn't either. It's about standing up for each other. Mrs. Squeak and Mr. Muscle haven't noticed yet. They have no imagination.

At supper Plum stuck her head between her fists. Dog felt the storm coming. The little girl clenched her jaw, and only the shortest words escaped her lips. "No. Not hungry. Don't want any. Don't care."

She was answering Mrs. Squeak's questions, Mr. Muscle's orders, and both their threats.

Plum ended up going to bed without swallowing a single mouthful or saying good night. But she glanced at Dog, giving him one of her special winks to let him know it wasn't his fault.

Something funny's going on, thinks Dog. He's lying on an old rag he pulled out of the kitchen cupboard because the tiles were too cold. And he's staring at his cold dinner with his nose tucked between his paws. Yes, come to think of it, there's been something funny going on for a while.

But Dog doesn't know what *exactly*. Mr. Muscle and Mrs. Squeak have been giving him shifty looks for two or three days now. And they keep talking in hushed whispers whenever Plum's around. Of course, Plum's noticed there's something funny going on. She's started giving her parents shifty looks back. So now they've stopped looking her in the eye altogether. They stammer and make the kind of silly excuses Plum gives her teachers when she pretends she's lost her backpack or forgotten her homework. Funny, isn't it?

Plum hasn't eaten anything for two whole days. What's going on? It's always bothered Dog that human beings are so unpredictable. They're not like dogs, who make their fur stand on end and stick their tail between their legs when they're in a bad mood. And they're not like cats, who usually let you know when their claws are coming out. And they're not like the weather either, which leaves lots of clues: changing smells, insects waking up, birds diving. . . . Human beings, on the other hand . . .

"Human beings . . ." he whispers. But he's lost the thread. His eyelids are growing heavy and he's drifting off. *"Time to sleep,"* he says. He tries opening an eye again, but he's already chasing a dream. *"All right,"* he sighs. And he nods off.

How Dog Was Born

Like all dogs, Dog's dreams make him relive the best moments of his life. And the worst. Everything gets played back to him, all jumbled up.

Like chasing seagulls on the beach . . .

Mr. Muscle is stretched out on the sand, and he's sneering. "Look at that beanpole! Can't catch a fly, but he'll never stop chasing those seagulls."

He's right, of course. But what Mr. Muscle doesn't realize is that Dog knows he'll never catch a seagull. And the seagulls know they're in no danger of being caught. It's just that Dog likes running after them along the surf where the waves break, and they like flying away from under his nose with a high-pitched mewing. Spurts of foam sparkle in the sunlight, and their white wings glisten against the blue sky. It's a beautiful game. Dog plays it every time he gets the chance, because up until now his life hasn't been a laughing matter.

And if he sobs and sighs as he sleeps in the kitchen, if he trembles from head to paw, it may be that he's remembering his puppyhood. Not a laughing matter at all.

Dog came from a family of five: three brothers, a sister, and him. Shortly after their birth a human voice from the sky crashed like thunder into their cardboard home.

"Let's see . . . three fives are fifteen, so that's five and one to carry; three ones are three, plus one makes four, which gives us forty-five; plus ten for the female, makes fifty-five. We'll make a tidy profit out of them."

And the voice added, "But not that one — he's too ugly. I can't see anyone wanting him. Better drown him."

And Dog was seized by an enormous hand, lifted to

a dizzy height, and dunked in a bucket of very cold water. He began to wriggle and groan and cry and choke. . . .

Just as he wriggles and cries and groans and chokes now in his dream.

Black Nose

What happened next? Had he fainted? To this day it remains a mystery. All Dog remembers are the sun's rays stroking him one morning, an overwhelming collection of smells, the whirl of seagulls in the sky, and a black nose next to him. It grunted as it scavenged among tin cans, burned-out tires, disemboweled mattresses, and shoes with holes in them.

"Ah! At last, you're opening your eyes!" said Black Nose, leaning over him. "And not a moment too soon. You're no beauty, are you? But you're certainly tough. It's rare to survive a dunking, you know."

Black Nose licked him affectionately and then went on. "That's right, make the most of the fact that your eyes are open now, and take a good look around. You need to learn quickly because I can't go on feeding you forever. I'm old and tired and I've suckled dozens of dogs before you, so don't go taking advantage of me. I mean it."

All the same, she gave him another lick and allowed him a mouthful of milk from a well-worn teat. The milk was rich and strong, with a distinctive taste of hazelnuts he would never forget.

Dog learned quickly. The dump outside town was a good school. It contained all the temptations and pleasures, not to mention the dangers, a dog might come across in life.

First, the smells. They crept around Dog, wafted above his head, snaked along and mingled together. So many smells, they drove him crazy. "Think hard," Black Nose would growl. "Concentrate."

Dog was trying to follow a smell of bacon rind with his nose to the ground. All of a sudden, without knowing how or why, he found himself on the trail of another smell, a strong whiff of fish that had ended its scaly life in a soup. Dog sat down with a bump, like all puppies do, because he was so confused.

"Are you daydreaming again?"

Dog went straight back to work, chasing a third smell. He lost his sense of direction, retraced his steps, walked around in circles, broke into a run, stopped short, took off again, and staggered like a drunk before falling asleep because he was so worn out. When he woke up, Black Nose was carefully licking his wounds.

"What a mess you are! You've grazed your nose on a tin can and cut yourself on a broken bottle. Why don't you look where you put your paws?"

Slowly Dog learned how to disentangle smells until he'd developed quite a talent for it. In fact, he soon had the best nose in the dump. Even the oldest dogs asked his advice.

"I was on the trail of a shinbone, the kind you find in beef stew, and I've just lost the scent. You wouldn't know where . . . ?"

"Behind the tractor tire over there, next to the typewriter," Dog would reply, without even waiting for the end of the question.

But the dump was also littered with dangers. Apart from all the things that could cut and sting and burn you, and the poisonous stuff, there were also rats and cats (luckily the cats tended to fight among themselves) and other dogs.

Generally speaking, a smell belonged to whoever sniffed it out first. If another dog had already followed a scent, he'd leave his own whiff on the original smell. So you had to find a new lead. Those were the rules. For a good lead (a mutton bone, for instance) you'd need to get up at the crack of dawn when the trucks were being unloaded and get to work right away. You had to watch out for lazy dogs who hated early starts and let everyone else do all the hard work before rolling up for the feast, fur on end, fangs out, and eyes blazing. They tried to take advantage of Dog a few times, but Black Nose intervened. All the dogs were in awe of her. She could reduce a thief to a shriveled cur, slinking off, head down, tail between his legs.

"I mean it!"

Black Nose wasn't very strong anymore, but she still had a reputation, and that's what counted.

The arrival of the garbage trucks was the most exciting and terrifying moment of the day. The avalanche of trash was so dangerous that many of the dogs steered clear. But Black Nose was adamant.

"If you want the best, there's only one way to get it: be there when they tip their loads, and keep your eyes peeled for what comes crashing down."

Down it crashed all right, and from a terrifying height.

"You won't see anything if you climb up there. Position yourself at the bottom, so the stuff has time to spread out. And watch out for blunt objects!"

"Blunt?"

"For anything metal or wood that's heavy enough to squash you. Just jump left or right, but don't forget to keep your eyes peeled for butchers' leftovers."

Black Nose had taught him how to jump. She was still deft and agile.

14 "Strength doesn't count for much in life. What matters is being able to dodge."

"Dodge?"

"Dodging. The knack of avoiding heavy blows. Watch out! There's a bed coming down!"

The bed crashed just behind them with a screeching of springs. Some mornings it felt as if the whole town were falling on your head. There were beds and cupboards and armchairs, as well as television sets that erupted like volcanoes on impact.

Black Nose taught Dog that no matter how careful you are, no one is safe from accidents. And no matter how happy you are, no one is safe from unhappiness. (It works the other way around too, of course.)

It was a clear summer's morning. The wind had been blowing all night. The sky was as clean as a well-licked stainless steel dish. Dog and Black Nose had risen very early with the sun. They were in a good mood. They enjoyed the summer, mainly because they liked the heat, but also because summer was the tourist season and the residents of the dump got to eat like kings — thanks to the restaurants.

Dog and Black Nose were waiting patiently at the edge of the dump. They could hear the distant hum of engines. Then a cloud of dust rose up behind the plane trees lining the road. The trucks loomed into sight; the avalanche followed.

How did it happen? An accident that was over in a flash. They'd dodged everything and located all the likely spots. But then a huge white metal object came tumbling out. It bounced off the heap and spun around heavily in the air.

"Watch out for that fridge!" warned Black Nose.

Dog laughed and leaped to one side as Black Nose

jumped forward to let the fridge land behind her. Which it did. But the door had worked itself loose in midflight. Black Nose didn't see it because it was hidden by the bulk of the fridge. It was the door that killed her. Dog thought it was a joke when he saw her laid out flat and panting. He ran around her, yapping and wiggling his behind.

"Stop fooling around," murmured Black Nose. "Not now . . ."

Dog stopped in his tracks and for the first time in his life felt an icy shiver run down his spine: Total Terror. Somehow he plucked up the courage to get close to her. Black Nose could only whisper now.

"If you go to the town," she said, "watch out for the cars. Dodge, little one, remember. . . ."

An Owner?

It's not a good idea to hang around the scene of a tragedy, thought Dog. You have to get going. But he realized something else too. I'll never be as happy again as I've been here.

The other dogs gathered around him. They let him weep and didn't say a word. Being there was all that mattered. The garbage trucks had gone and only Dog's sobbing broke the silence. High above the dump a train went past with a long plaintive whistle. Why did Black Nose talk to me about the town? Dog wondered through his tears. In all the time he'd known her, Black Nose had mentioned the town only two or three times.

One day he'd asked her, "Have you ever lived in the town?"

"Yes."

Silence.

"Was it fun?"

"It had good points and bad points, just like everything else."

Silence.

"Why didn't you stay there? How come you moved to the dump?"

Black Nose hesitated. A shadow crept across her eyes. And then she gave a peculiar answer. "Because, as my owner used to say, you can't live in the present if you're tied to the past."

Dog tried to understand, and then he burst out, "You used to have an owner?"

"A mistress, yes."

"Was she nice?"

Black Nose fell silent. When she replied, it was in a different voice, full of memories and tenderness and companionship, tinged with sadness. "Very!" And then she added proudly, "I trained her well. . . ."

Perhaps that was why Black Nose had mentioned the town before she died. So that Dog would go and find a mistress, and spend his dog's life at her side. He looked around the dump at all the dogs gathered there.

They weren't a very glamorous bunch, with their ripped ears and bandy legs, their bald patches and baggy eyes, their lonely expressions and all their fleas hopping around in the sunshine.

"All right, Black Nose," he promised, "I'll go to the town and I'll find a mistress."

None of his friends were surprised when he cut through their circle, climbed the hill beside the dump, and headed off along the road lined with plane trees. He was still sobbing, but he never looked back. Not once.

"When you've made a decision, never go back on it," Black Nose had advised him. "Hesitation is a dog's worst enemy."

19

The Town

If Dog's legs twitch now in his dream, if he pants like a seal, if his heart beats rapidly, it's because he's heading into town. It's a journey he remembers vividly. . . .

The town was a long way off. But it wasn't difficult to find. Dog just had to follow the tunnel of smells carved out of the morning air by the garbage trucks on their way home. Whenever a car came toward him, Dog jumped to the side: dodging. Then he moved on through the tunnel of smells. He walked in quick puppy steps, and his little legs looked like four knitting needles. He didn't stop to draw breath. But he'd managed to stop crying. Dog couldn't think about anything except reaching the town and finding a mistress, as Black Nose had suggested.

All of a sudden the tunnel of smells split in two. Dog hesitated for a moment before turning left. He walked with his nose at road level. The tunnel divided again. This time he turned right. Then left again, then right. Eventually he realized the tunnel had come to an end because the smells were spreading out in every direction. He lifted his head and sat back before sticking out his tongue as far as he could and taking in a great gulp of air. He was in the town center.

It was a very big town. Lots of buildings and cars (he definitely had a knack for dodging by now) as well as tourists and locals. With so many people around, it wouldn't be difficult to find an owner. But first things first. He was hungry. Dog lifted his nose and sniffed slowly, flaring his nostrils as widely as he could. Forty different smells rushed in at once. He recognized each of them. They were fresher, of course, but otherwise exactly the same as at the dump.

So that's what a town is. . . . It's just a dump that's bigger and more spread out and fresher smelling!

Dog sifted through the smells one by one, discarding rubber, gas, oranges, flowers, and shoes. All of a sudden his right nostril flared, his left eyebrow shot up, and he began to drool. He'd found a mouth-watering smell of meat. And it was close by, which was even better. There had to be a butcher's shop somewhere in the area.

As it turned out, the butcher's shop was just across the street. But the butcher looked as if he weighed at least two hundred pounds. He was terrifying. He had knives everywhere, and his apron was as big as a billboard. He was standing on the doorstep, his fists like clubs on his hips.

Black Nose's words echoed in Dog's memory. "Don't trust human beings — they're unpredictable."

He watched the butcher on the pavement opposite. By now saliva was trickling down Dog's legs. That whiff of fresh meat was making him starving hungry. Every so often a passing car would hide the butcher. Dog wished he would disappear by the time the car moved on. But it was no use: the butcher was still there, and he looked more terrifying than ever. The smell was still there too, in Dog's nostrils. It had chased all the other smells away. And Dog's saliva had made a pool on the pavement.

The smell, the butcher, the butcher, the smell . . .

I have to make up my mind, thought Dog. And he remembered Black Nose's advice. "Think carefully before you make a decision, and never go back on it."

Dog tried to concentrate. As he watched the butcher carefully, he noticed something. The butcher's apron didn't hang low enough to cover the gap between his long legs. The gap was just wide enough for a dog his size to squeeze through.

I'll race across the road and barge through his legs. Then I'll grab the first bit of meat I find and scram. He's fat and I'm fast, so he won't catch me. With a bit of luck he won't even notice anything's happened.

It didn't work out that way, of course. He'd barely reached the middle of the road when several scary things happened at once. Someone shouted, Dog froze to the spot, and then the butcher came rushing toward him, waving his red hands. Before he knew it, Dog was pinned against that vast chest, and the butcher's voice was exploding in his ears.

"The nerve! You city types are all the same! Think you can come here and run over our dogs? Move it before I lose my temper!"

There was a screeching of tires, and the car set off again. The car that had almost run Dog over.

The butcher held Dog at arm's length and looked him straight in the eye. "Got a name? Going to tell us where you're from? You're not very handsome, are you? Bet you're hungry though."

And that was that. The butcher gave Dog a magnificent bone covered with meat and left him to gnaw it on the sawdust in the middle of the shop. He even gave Dog plenty of time to digest his meal. Dog fell asleep listening to the butcher telling his customers the story.

"City slicker. What a nerve, coming here and running over our dogs. I told him to move it or I'd lose my temper. . . ."

When Dog woke up, several hours later, the butcher was lowering the iron shutter in front of his shop. Before locking up, he turned to Dog.

"Made up your mind, then? Are you coming or going?"

Dog went to him. What a shame he was looking for a mistress, not a master. He scratched at the iron shutter with his paw.

"You want out? Well, I hope you have a nice life. . . ." There wasn't a trace of anger in the butcher's voice. And he didn't sound sad either. His tone seemed to say, "To each his own, I reckon. It's a free world." Then he added in a much more serious voice, "Have you learned your lesson? Don't go getting run over!"

Beware of Rats

If they're all like him in this town, thought Dog as he left the butcher's shop, it won't be difficult to find a mistress. He began following the first passerby as if he'd known her all his life. The passerby had long thin legs. She smelled of violets, and her heels went *tip-tap* just as Mrs. Squeak's would later do.

It took the passerby a while to realize she was being followed. She stopped in front of a store, and Dog came to a halt at her feet. She glued her nose to the store window, and he did the same a bit lower down. She looked longingly at the merchandise, and he sniffed some smells approvingly.

We should get along well, Dog thought. After all, we like doing the same things.

The passerby set off again and so did Dog, wagging his tail, his nose barely an inch from her heels. They carried on like this until the passerby stopped in front of a fruit stand. Dog didn't like fruit very much, but the smells at ground level were more interesting — wonderful green smells left there by country dogs. The passerby chose a plump peach, and Dog settled on a subtle kind of smell. When the passerby opened her purse to pay, Dog lifted his paw to keep her company. And that was the beginning of the end.

"Is that your pooch?" shouted the grocer, thrusting his crimson head over the counter.

"Certainly not!" protested the passerby.

"So how come he's been following you from the bottom of the road?"

"I've never seen him before in my life." (The passerby was getting politely annoyed.)

"Try telling that to him!" The grocer bared his teeth. "And that'll be ten dollars for the crate of peaches he's just messed up with his paw!"

"I beg your pardon? Someone call the police!" shrieked the passerby, who was on the verge of fainting.

"Fine by me," agreed the grocer. "Police!" he shouted, leaping into the street.

As everyone knows, the police are always there when you need them.

"Does this dog belong to you?" asked the first officer, getting out his pencil.

"She's too cheap to pay for the peaches. That's why she won't admit it," jeered the grocer.

"We'll deal with you in a minute, mister grocer," said the second officer, getting out his notebook.

"I'm telling you — it's not my dog," sobbed the passerby.

"Which dog are we talking about anyway?" asked the first policeman.

Because there were now at least a dozen dogs sitting outside the shop. The argument was great entertainment, and the audience had already started laying bets.

"Bet you a chicken drumstick it'll end in a brawl," said the old boxer from the shoe store next door.

"The cops'll arrest everybody," predicted the baker's spitz, who liked to think he'd been around the block a few times.

"Really," drawled the antique dealer's greyhound. "A lot of fuss about nothing."

And then a voice from the sky said, "Hey, Great Dane, I saw you peeing on the peaches!" It belonged to the colonel's Chihuahua, who was on his balcony and up to his old tricks of teasing the insurance broker's Great Dane.

The Great Dane gave his usual reply. "Come down here, you silly little twit! Call yourself a dog? Come down if you've got something to say!"

Meanwhile, Dog (our dog) had slipped away. Looking for a mistress in the street isn't the right way of going about things, he said to himself. There are too many people around. You need a little privacy to get to know someone.

No sooner had this idea occurred to him than Dog found himself in front of an open door with a strong smell of fish soup wafting out of it. The room he wandered into had no people in it. Again he recognized the dump. This time it was the furniture that was the same. Except that the hutch, sofa, television, and dresser were all in reasonable condition and had been sensibly placed against the walls.

So that's what a house is, Dog thought. It's a dump that's been cleaned up.

Dog decided to lie down near the sofa while he waited for someone to turn up. He also decided to pretend he was asleep to make himself look more at home.

He tucked his nose between his paws but kept an eye open for the first person to come in.

It was a big blonde lady with a fresh face and shiny cheeks. Her sleeves were rolled up, showing her pink arms, and she wiggled her round hips when she walked. She smelled of freshly washed plates, and her two tiny blue eyes blinked behind an enormous pair of glasses.

Seems nice enough, thought Dog.

She didn't see him at first. She bent over the counter and stood up again with a pile of plates in her arms. She turned and headed toward the table in the middle of the room. Halfway there she stopped. She seemed to hesitate for a moment before turning around and staring hard with those tiny eyes. Then she scrunched her nose, wrinkled her forehead, and opened her mouth wide. She'd just caught sight of Dog. The pile of plates smashed to the ground with a terrible clatter. This caught Dog by surprise, making him jump right onto the sofa, and by the time he landed, the fat lady had leaped onto a chair.

"A rat!" she screamed. "A rat! Leon, come quickly! There's a rat! Quickly! Quiiiiickly!"

A rat? Dog was puzzled. Where? And his fur bristled with excitement all over his body, because he wasn't scared of rats. If he could begin life with his new mistress by catching a rat, he'd be off to a flying start. So he tried to make himself look as intimidating as possible. He rolled back his lips to reveal a set of narrow canines as sharp and shiny as steel needles. The big lady moved from the chair to the table.

"Leon, please, come quickly! Quickly! He's enormous, enoooormous!"

Leon couldn't have weighed more than ninety pounds, but he was armed with a broom, and he had a mean look in his eyes.

"Where? Where?" he shouted, bursting into the room.

"There, on the sofa," the blonde lady shrieked, pointing a wobbly finger at Dog.

Dog escaped the first swing of the broom by the skin of his teeth. He dodged the second too, and the third. He was running around the room, jumping right and left the way Black Nose had taught him, while the broom handle broke a vase of flowers, smashed the telephone, and shattered two window panes in a single blow. In the end Dog decided to head off, because he'd never be able to convince these two nut cases he wasn't a rat.

Night had long since fallen over the town. The houses had swallowed up their inhabitants. The cars had fallen asleep beside the sidewalks. Dog walked alone in the middle of the streets. The yellow glow of the streetlights made his shadow look very black. If only I'd known, thought Dog, I'd have stayed at the butcher's. Human beings really *were* unpredictable. You couldn't be sure of anything when they were involved. The smells had gone to sleep too. They hovered at ground level, which is the way smells sleep, moving about ever so slightly. The sea breeze wrapped them in a salty blanket.

Dog walked as if in a dream. His paws didn't make a sound. He felt sleepy now. He chose the most comfortable tub of flowers in Garibaldi Square, made a bed for himself among the geraniums, turned around six times, and let out a sigh as he rolled up into a ball. But before he went to sleep, he had to decide what he was going to do next. He pondered a little while longer. A clock chimed midnight in the old part of town.

That's it, decided Dog. Tomorrow I'm going back to the butcher's. He's not a mistress, but I'm sure Black Nose would approve. Anyway, who knows? He might even be married. . . .

What a Way to Wake Up

Dog woke up with the sun. Getting up early was a habit he'd learned at the dump and one he'd never lose. The town was waking up gently. It looked very pretty, with its geraniums and its orange trees, and its houses painted in shades of ocher and sky blue. The smells were already beginning to rise skyward.

Dog was trying to track down the butcher's smell. It took him a while to find it again because he'd strayed a long way when he'd followed the passerby. He discounted the first smell of a specialty-meats butcher and the second of a butcher selling artificially fattened meat; he hovered over a third, a delicatessen; and eventually he settled on the last, which was a long way off but still the strongest. It was a healthy whiff of meat that had been fed on plenty of fresh grass and freedom, and Dog recognized the butcher's personal smell.

Dog had immediately noticed the delicate fragrance of lavender when the butcher had held him to his chest. "So what?" you might say. "Lots of people smell of lavender." Which is true. But there aren't lots of butchers who smell of lavender. They smell of parsley, mostly. This strong whiff of meat from the meadows mixed with the delicate fragrance of lavender could only be his butcher. So Dog set off, his nose in the air, alert as ever.

34 He walked into the wind so as not to lose the trail. He took no notice of what was going on around him.

"Don't allow yourself to be distracted when you're following a trail," whispered Black Nose somewhere in his memory.

But the sights and sounds around Dog were interesting. Housekeepers were sweeping their doorsteps while garbage trucks swallowed trash bags through the jaws in their behinds. And what jaws! They gobbled up anything and everything, from meat and clothes to shoes and plastic wrapping, crunching them all to the sound of clanging of metal. And while the trucks munched their breakfast, street sweepers went rolling past on cushioned brushes, whizzing around at high speed and sending out spurts of water in every direction. The town was having its morning wash. It was a tourist town, and the mayor wanted it to be spick-and-span every day of the week.

"These people certainly know how to declare war on smells," muttered Dog, trying not to lose the scent of his butcher's shop.

He was concentrating ten times harder than usual. Which is why he didn't hear the gray van. Not that it made any noise. It had been following him for some time now, coasting along beside the pavement. It was as silent as a snake and just as dangerous. When the net came swooping down, it was too late.

"And another one!"

Dog bit the hand that grabbed him, but it was protected by a thick leather glove. An iron door opened. Dog was thrown into a black hole. The door slammed shut. The driver started up the engine.

In the Dog Pound

"So you got nabbed too?" piped up a voice in the darkness.

It took Dog a while to make out who was talking to him.

"You're only a pup," the voice went on. "Couldn't you have given them the slip?"

"That's *precisely* my point," sniffed a disapproving voice. "Young dogs today . . . haven't a clue. Never look where they're going, and before they know it, they end up behind bars."

"So how come *you're* in here if you're so clever?" asked the first voice wearily.

"Special case," sniffed the second voice. "They caught me while I was asleep. But they won't keep me long. First chance I get, I'm out of here."

"Yeah . . . yeah . . . that's what they all say," the first voice continued. It belonged to a large pile of wool lying at the back of the van. "But it's getting more difficult."

"Where are we going?" Dog finally plucked up the courage to ask the woolly one.

"I don't believe my ears!" said Sniffy. "Were you born in a barn, my friend? What have I done to be locked up with a halfwit like you?"

"Leave him alone," growled Woolly, his teeth gleaming in the half-darkness. Then he turned toward Dog. "They're taking us to the dog pound."

"Why?" asked Dog, who also wanted to know what a dog pound was but didn't dare ask too many questions at once.

"Why? Oh, *please*! Someone pinch me; I must be dreaming." And Sniffy began whispering in Dog's ear. "Municipal by-law of July 1 of this year: 'Regarding the need for cleaning up our town, and taking into consideration the proliferation of stray dogs threatening our tourist industry, the rounding up of the said dogs by the relevant council authorities will henceforth be carried out on a daily basis. If the owners concerned do not reclaim their pets WITHIN A PERIOD OF THREE DAYS' — bang! bang!

"The last two words are my own," whispered Sniffy with a horrible grin. "They don't sound official, but they mean the same thing."

There was a deathly hush. The van spluttered as it edged forward. From time to time the engine cut out, and they coasted along, braking gently. Sometimes the van stopped with a jolt, and the back door opened to reveal the shadow of a dog being hurled inside.

"There must be some mistake! Do you realize who you're dealing with?" shouted one of the newcomers, much to Sniffy's amusement.

Sometimes the new arrivals were half asleep and didn't bother kicking up a fuss. Sometimes they just said, "Hi, guys! How long?"

"Three days," Woolly would reply.

And Sniffy would add, "Or else — bang! bang!"

But every so often the van started its engine again without the door having been thrown open. At which point there was a general hullabaloo, with Sniffy shouting louder than everyone else. "Missed! Missed!

What a bunch of losers! Fire them all! Call yourselves dogcatchers? Tortoise chasers, more like. Miiissed! Miiissed! Paaathetic! Try your luck with snails! Or slugs! Miiiiiissed! Miiiiiissed!"

Even Woolly joined in. And then the noise began to die down until it finally stopped altogether.

Because, all things considered, there wasn't much to shout about.

Total Terror

The dog pound is Dog's worst memory. At this point in his dream, he always starts shouting out in the night. This in turn makes Mr. Muscle wake up with a jolt and start complaining. "Dog's dreaming again! I can't put up with much more of this." Actually, Mr. Muscle's frightened. His blood runs cold when that whining sound rises from Dog's memory. So Mr. Muscle wakes Mrs. Squeak because he doesn't like feeling frightened.

"What? What is it? What's going on?"

"It's Dog. He's dreaming," whispers Mr. Muscle.

"Again?" squeaks Mrs. Squeak. "I really can't stand much more of this."

As for Plum, she's sleeping so deeply, she wouldn't hear a gun being fired.

And Dog is shut in the kitchen. Alone with his dream. Alone with his memories.

There was such a racket when they arrived at the dog pound. The metal hangar with its concrete floor made their voices ring out.

The dogs who were already there rushed up to the bars of their cages. The sound of barking broke out everywhere.

"Take a good look, lads. It's the new boys!"

"Kind of you to join us!"

"Well, fancy that, if it isn't our old friend Sniffy! **41** Got yourself picked up again, misery guts?"

"Three days! Three days!"

"Long live the mayor!"

And so on, just to show they weren't frightened. But things soon went quiet, just as they had in the van. Because beyond their silence and hidden under several layers of pride lurked Total Terror, the same fear that Dog had experienced in front of Black Nose's motionless body. He felt it in all the hushed conversations around him.

"I'm not hanging around," said one voice. "It's just a matter of a quick identity check."

"I'll bite anyone who touches me!" growled another.

"Frankly, I couldn't give a hoot. . . . It's a dog's life, whatever happens. . . ."

And the worst thing was, none of them believed a word they were saying.

Some whined for hours on end.

"And they talk about cleaning up the town? They've got nerve, making out we're the ones polluting it. What about all the exhaust fumes we have to breathe in from their stinking cars? They say we've got rabies, but what about their crazy fits of road rage? The day before yesterday, I saw two drivers attack each other over a parking space —"

"Crazy? They're stark raving mad," interrupted another voice. "Last week one actually bit me!"

This raised a few laughs here and there.

"It's true, I swear! He was a friend of my owner's. So up I trotted, held out my paw and . . . OUCH!"

"Hey, that's enough. Shut up!"

Silence. Total Terror was on the prowl, and no one really wanted to talk anyway. Each dog was worried about the future.

*   *   *

The hours went by. Those who had owners jumped up each time the main gate opened. They glued their noses to the bars. Sometimes an owner did arrive, and everyone was forced to witness the reunion. The dogs would jump up and down on the ends of leashes, and the owners kept repeating their pets' names. They looked like long-lost lovers when the owners kissed and hugged the dogs, who licked them back.

"They're pedigrees, of course," remarked Woolly. (Dog, Woolly, and the rest of the gang from the van had all been locked up in the same cage.)

"What's a pedigree?" asked Dog.

"It's an idea invented by humans," replied Sniffy scornfully, "and it's completely fake. For example, you might take a very fast dog like the greyhound, a very muscular dog like the Alsatian, and a very hardy dog like the beagle. Mix them all together and what do you get? The Doberman. Once you've bred a Doberman, he's allowed to marry only other Dobermans. Human beings love Dobermans, but I think they're idiots. I've known quite a few in my time and I can tell you it wasn't a Doberman who invented the shinbone! Hardly surprising, when you think how much they intermarry. They have nasty dispositions, and they're so stuck up —"

"All right, you've made your point," interrupted Woolly. "I once had a friend who was a Doberman, and he was very nice too."

"There's always the odd exception," admitted Sniffy, "but by and large . . ."

"Are you a pedigree?" Dog asked Woolly.

Woolly managed a feeble smile. "I have every kind of pedigree in me. I'm related to any dog you care to mention. Even Sniffy here, who doesn't look a bit like me. Even you . . ."

"Don't you have an owner?"

The smile vanished from Woolly's face. A long silence followed. A very long silence indeed. Finally Woolly said, "I used to have a mistress. . . ."

Silence.

"And?"

Silence.

"I lost her."

The sun was high in the sky. It was stiflingly hot under the great metal roof of the dog pound. There were a lot of tongues hanging out.

"What d'you mean, lost her?"

"Just that. I went out for a walk one evening and

when I came back the next morning, she was gone. The apartment was empty. She'd moved out."

"Typical," snorted Sniffy. "She probably found herself a new man. He didn't like dogs, and in a tossup between the two of you, he won hands down."

"Perhaps," said Woolly.

"But didn't you follow her smell?" asked Dog, amazed.

"What good would it have done? If she didn't want me anymore, what was the point?"

"Quite right not to go crawling after her," applauded Sniffy. "We dogs have our self-respect to consider."

After a while Woolly said in a thoughtful voice, "Anyway, it's my fault. I didn't train her properly —"

Their conversation was interrupted by something Dog would never forget. Something that's made him call out every night ever since. The main gate swung open onto the setting sun. A black van reversed through the gate into the dog pound. Ten men wearing leather gloves jumped out. They opened a whole row of cages, grabbed hold of the dogs, and hurled them into the van. The director of the dog pound watched the whole operation with a blank smile on his face.

The dogs were kicking with all four legs and barking and biting. But it was over in a flash, and nothing they did made any difference. The van took off again. The gates closed behind it.

There was a deathly silence. A gust of Total Terror had just blown through. All the dogs were looking at the row of empty cages. They were the day-three cages.

Sniffy

The next day Dog and his friends were moved to a day-two cage. They had another day of waiting ahead of them. In the small hours a new supply of stray dogs had been put in their old cage. There was the same ker-fuffle as the day before when they'd first arrived. And the day panned out just the same. Except there was more tension. The sun grew hotter as it climbed over the corrugated iron roof, until the heat became unbear-able. The water in the tin trays was tepid. None of the dogs touched their food. From time to time an owner would come to pick up a dog. But for every dog rescued, there were lots more dashed hopes.

Toward three o'clock in the afternoon a strange procession arrived. In front was a tall blonde girl who lisped loudly. Behind her a hairy man with a beard was carrying a black machine with an eye on one end. And in third place was the pound director, smiling blankly.

As soon as they were in view, all the dogs began to bark in unison.

"Journalists! Journalists! Yoo-hoo! Over here, journalists! Me! Me! No, not him, meeee!"

"What's going on?" Dog asked Woolly.

"It's for TV. They have a slot for homeless dogs. They come here once a week and choose a dog to film for the local news, to help find a new owner."

"And what do you have to do to be filmed?" asked Dog.

"Be good-looking."

"They'll probably pick you," said Dog. "You're very handsome."

"Thank you," sighed Woolly, "but I'm too old. You also have to be young, and not too fat."

"Young and not too fat? Like me, for example? D'you think they'd choose me?"

"You have *got* to be joking!" sneered Sniffy. "Have you seen your face? You're *much* too ugly. But I'm *exactly* what they're looking for." And, pushing Dog out of the way, he glued himself to the cage.

What happened next had to be seen to be believed. Sniffy (who was completely stuck up and never had a good word to say about anyone, who made fun of "doggy-woggies and their mollycoddling owners," who'd just spent two days talking about independence and freedom and self-respect) now glued his entire body to the cage and whimpered in a voice that was soft and musical and not the slightest bit arrogant.

"Hey! You journalists! *Please* will you listen? I'm a poor homeless dog whose mistress died. . . . Don't you feel sorry for me? Couldn't you find me another home, with lots of kiddy-widdies to play with? I'm a complete natural with children. I love them to bits."

It was so convincing (and so different from all the other clamorings) that the blonde journalist stopped in front of the cage with tears in her eyes.

"Oh, he's so cute," she sobbed. "Don't you think he's cute, Coco? He's to die for. And *soooo* handsome. I'm sure he has some long-haired dachshund in him. He'd make an adorable dog for a condo owner, wouldn't he? Don't you think, Coco?"

Coco was the hairy man with the beard. He was struggling with a very heavy camera. The sweat was pouring off him. He agreed.

*   *   *

Two hours later, once the filming was over, they brought Sniffy back. He was very pleased, and his fur was all glossy and shiny.

"It was absolutely fantastic: makeup, lights, a velvet cushion . . . the whole works. The only thing was, they filmed me with some kind of cat, an angora or something, which stank of perfume and had a ludicrous silk bow tied around its neck. I was dying to attack it. If I clap eyes on that cat when I get out . . ."

50   There was a hush. Everyone found his behavior embarrassing, but Sniffy didn't seem to notice. He just babbled on.

"Couldn't be easier, really. First thing tomorrow my owners-to-be will come for me. There'll be at least fifty, I imagine. And I'll just have to choose between them. The kids are the only snag. Can't stand the brats. They really get on my nerves. Not that it matters much. As soon as my new owners turn their backs, I'll be off again. Freedom and self-respect, you see . . ."

He talked and he talked. Nobody listened. The sun was setting. They tried not to look in the direction of the main gate, which was about to open.

The Lobster, the Turnip, and the Sun

Sure enough, they came for Sniffy the next day. There were at least ten would-be owners arguing over him. One group claimed they'd arrived first, but another insisted *no, they had*. They looked as if they were going to start hitting each other.

After they left with Sniffy, it got quiet again. All the dogs could do was wait. Woolly and Dog were in a day-three cage. They stayed there all day long. The sun set on their fading hopes.

"Time to be brave," said Woolly.

"Yes," said Dog, nuzzling against his companion's thick curly fur.

The main gate opened.

"That's it, then," said Woolly.

"Yes," said Dog, burying his head in Woolly's coat.

"Chin up," Woolly scolded him gently. "When the going gets tough, you've got to be brave."

Dog raised his head. He was sitting, tucked between Woolly's paws. Both of them were staring at the gate. It gaped onto a bloodstained sunset.

But no black van appeared. Instead, three people walked in. A tall man in shorts, red as a lobster and very angry. A skinny woman in a flowery hat, white as a turnip and very angry. And, in between the two of them, the most extraordinary sight Dog had ever seen: a little girl, absolutely tiny. Her red hair was straight as straw and it shone like rays of sunlight around her head. She had two teeny-weeny clenched fists. And an enormous mouth that was wide open and shouting.

"I WANT A DOG!"

Behind the three visitors stood the manager of the dog pound with a blank smile on his face.

"Who on earth are they?" growled Woolly.

The answer erupted from all the cages at the same time. "Tourists!"

The word *tourists* was enough to make the whole dog pound explode with fury.

"Down with tourists!"

"Beat it!"

"It's your fault we're here!"

"They passed the by-law of July 1 because of you!"

"Anyone care for a bit of tourist for supper?"

But one cry rose above all the noise, and it belonged to the little red ball of sunshine.

"I WANT A DOG!"

"No need to shout. You'll get your dog," groaned the giant lobster.

"There are doggies all around you, my pet," squeaked the flowery turnip.

"I WANT A DOG!"

"Of course, we understand. Mommy and Daddy are going to choose one for you."

"NO! I WANT TO CHOOSE ONE!"

"All right, all right, *you* choose. Don't you think that one's cute? He looks like a poodle."

"I DON'T WANT A POODLE!"

All this shouting petrified the dogs, and then it drove them crazy. Some hurled themselves against their cages, others banged their heads against the walls, and all of them barked.

"We've had enough!"

"Shut her up!"

"Stop torturing us!"

"Turn down the volume!"

"Down, little girl! Heel!"

But, above it all: "I DON'T WANT A FOX TERRIER!"

Only Woolly and Dog remained silent. The cries of the miniature red sun pierced their ears and set their teeth on edge, but they kept quiet. They watched the trio approaching, as Dog disappeared even farther between Woolly's legs.

All of a sudden, there they were, in front of the cage.

"I WANT THAT ONE!"

"That big woolly sheepdog?" exclaimed the flowery turnip. "What a good idea. He's magnificent. Don't you think, dear?"

"He could be a giraffe for all I care, as long as we get out of here," replied the king-size lobster, who wasn't even looking.

"NO, NOT THAT ONE — THIS ONE!" Her little finger trembled as she pointed to Dog.

"WHAT? THAT UGLY BRUTE?" shrilled the flowery turnip.

"YES, THAT ONE."

"ABSOLUTELY NOT!"

"IT'S THE ONLY ONE I WANT!"

"NEVER!"

When she was angry, the flowery turnip's voice was as terrifying as her daughter's. But Dog wasn't listening. He'd turned his back, tucked his head down, and hidden against Woolly's belly. His words came tumbling out between clenched teeth.

"I don't want to go. I don't ever want to leave you. Don't let them take me away."

"Don't be silly," replied Woolly, trying to hide his feelings. "This is your only chance, and I'm not going to let you mess it up."

"No, I'm not leaving you!" shouted Dog. And he leaped wildly at the cage, baring his small teeth as if he meant to devour all three of them.

"AND TO TOP IT OFF, HE BITES!" roared the flowery turnip as she took a leap backward.

"COOL! COOL! HE BITES! I WANT A BAD DOG! I WANT *THAT* ONE!"

My Very Own Dog

So they took him away with them. The scary little red sun stood her ground, despite a violent outburst from the enraged turnip. And in desperation the king-size lobster was finally forced to intervene.

"Let her take the dog, for goodness' sake! Or she'll go on a hunger strike again."

The cage opened. The director of the dog pound leaned in and smiled his blank smile. Dog kicked with his legs and resisted with his teeth. But Woolly pushed him outside with one nudge of his nose.

So Dog gave up the struggle. He sobbed quietly in the arms of the red sun, who suddenly changed into the kindest little girl. She kept stroking him and saying, over and over again, "He's MY dog. He's MY dog. He's MY VERY OWN dog."

Dog was far too upset to grasp that what she was saying might be alarming. He just kept on sobbing. He thought he would sob like that forever. But sadness is a strange thing. Even when you're grief-stricken, you notice things that have nothing to do with being upset. So while he was crying because he'd lost Woolly, Dog noticed the little girl smelled of plums, which was a strange thing to smell of because plums weren't in season yet. But Dog would soon learn that seasons and time didn't exist for his new owner. She got whatever she wanted, the moment she wanted it. That afternoon she must have fancied a plum. And this evening she wanted a dog.

The main gate opened wide. All the dogs barked their heads off as the trio of tourists left. Suddenly a black shadow darkened the dog pound. The barking petered out. Beneath the shadow blew a gust of Total Terror.

A Well-Trained Owner

Dog always wakes up at this point in his dream. He's just seen the black van, and the last look Woolly gave him. Dog opens his eyes. He's been woken by the sound of his own whimpering. This time Plum wakes up too.

It's not Dog's whimpering that has made her stir, but something inside her saying, "Wake up! Dog's upset!" She runs out of her bedroom, rushes into the kitchen, and picks up a trembling Dog. She walks barefoot on the kitchen tiles, even though she's not supposed to. She takes Dog into her bedroom, even though it's out of bounds. She tucks him up beside her in bed, even though it's strictly forbidden. And then she begins whispering, very gently, in his ear.

"Was it that nightmare again? Don't worry, Dog; I'm here now. I'll never leave you. Never!"

She whispers until Dog is so relaxed, he falls asleep again. He's proud of himself too. Black Nose and Woolly would approve: Plum is a good owner. Dog trained her well.

It hasn't been easy, mind you.

Not easy at all. . . .

Hooray for Seagulls!

The first few days went smoothly. Plum had made up her mind to comfort Dog, who sobbed from morning to night. And when Plum decided on something . . .

She never left Dog's side. She squeezed him against her chest and spoke tenderly to him. It wasn't the same voice she'd used at the dog pound. It was a voice that came from *inside* her. And when Dog heard it, he felt as if he was actually *inside* Plum, her words wrapping him in a warm, humming blanket.

Little by little he stopped crying. She took him to the beach. He chased the seagulls.

"Look at that beanpole!" Mr. Muscle sneered.

"Can't catch a fly, but he'll never stop chasing those seagulls! Stupid animals, dogs."

And then Mr. Muscle decided it was his turn to get up and start running. He didn't chase anything. He just ran, squatted down, stretched out his arms, took a few deep breaths, got up, and started running all over again. He kept it up for hours on end. When he finished his workout, he lay down next to Mrs. Squeak. He seemed very pleased with himself. Goodness knows why.

"You're soaking again," said Mrs. Squeak crossly.

She was right: he never went swimming, but he was always dripping wet from head to toe.

"Got to keep trim!" he replied, trying to make his head touch his knees.

Running to keep fit and sweating like a waterfall made Mr. Muscle give off a peculiar smell. The upshot was that Dog never got too close to Mr. Muscle. And he didn't get too close to Mrs. Squeak either. Because, while Mr. Muscle was developing his muscles and body odor with all that running, jumping, and sweating, Mrs. Squeak spent all day long getting a peculiar bottle out of her handbag and spraying herself with it. The first time, Dog was sitting right next to her. She got the bottle out, unscrewed a ludicrously complicated lid, and started spraying everywhere: head, shoulders, even behind her ears. When a few drops fell on Dog's nose, he suffered a terrible sneezing fit. He was sneezing so violently, he thought he'd die. His nostrils felt like they'd been sprinkled with pepper.

"What's the matter? What's going on? For goodness' sake, stop sneezing! Yuck! These animals are so *unhygienic!*" squeaked Mrs. Squeak.

She squeaked so loudly, Dog ran to hide behind Plum's legs.

"What have you done to MY dog?" asked Plum in a flash, and her voice spelled trouble.

"I haven't done anything to him, my pet! He's the one who keeps spluttering all over me. It's disgusting!"

"My dog isn't disgusting," said Plum with a strange glint in her eye. "I don't advise anyone to call MY dog disgusting!"

And then she started chasing after the seagulls with Dog. They looked like splashes of silver in the sky, and their wings gleamed white. It was a beautiful sight. Dog ran and jumped. But sometimes, instead of a seagull flying away, he saw something else against the blue sky. Something white and heavy that was made of metal and spun round as it fell. Dog would stop in his tracks and let out a long wail, just as he had done in front of Black Nose's corpse. Then he'd remember the last look Woolly had given him, and he'd carry on wailing until Plum took him in her arms, squeezed him against her chest, and let him hear the warm voice inside her.

Dog Gets a Name

The day Dog got his name was another happy memory from those early days.

That particular evening, friends from the campsite had gathered together around Mr. Muscle and Mrs. Squeak's caravan. (Mr. Muscle, Mrs. Squeak, and Plum always spent their summer vacation at this campsite, which wasn't far from town.)

The heat was suffocating, but they insisted on lighting a fire, to make it more of a party. Dog didn't think it made it more of a party. He just thought it was too hot. They lined up four or five tables end to end, covered them with food, and planted a forest of bottles on them. Everybody was sitting around the tables, and Dog was sitting on Plum's lap. Plum had the seat of honor, which was probably why Mr. Muscle kept calling her "my little princess."

And it was probably because of the bottles that everyone kept singing louder and louder. Dog didn't think their voices sounded tuneful. He thought they were too loud. It gave him the jitters. He'd never seen or heard so many human beings all at once. He tried to make himself as small as possible on Plum's lap, so they'd forget about him. But it didn't work.

All of a sudden Mr. Muscle raised his glass very high and bellowed, "Call me old-fashioned, but I reckon we should christen this mongrel!" ("This mongrel" meant Dog.)

"Good idea! Good idea! Let's give him a name!" bawled the guests, who always agreed with Mr. Muscle.

Plum squeezed Dog a bit more tightly.

"What do you think, my little princess?"

"I'll have to see." She shrugged. "What kind of name are you suggesting?"

Everyone suddenly went very quiet. No one had the faintest idea. Well . . . um . . . actually . . . as a matter of . . . what kind of name? And for the first time in his life, Dog saw human beings *thinking*. It was an interesting sight. They started off looking at one another, cocking their eyebrows and hunching their shoulders; then they pinched their chins and stared into space; then they scratched their heads and shuffled their feet; and finally they all turned back to Mr. Muscle to ask him if he'd come up with anything yet.

"I'm still thinking," Mr. Muscle replied.

And so everyone set to thinking again.

Dog was beginning to enjoy the evening's entertainment. Mr. Muscle was very funny when he was thinking. He wrinkled his forehead like a bulldog and stuck out his lower jaw. Dog almost expected to hear his brain fizzing and popping. Mr. Muscle had turned an even deeper shade of red than usual. All the guests fell quiet as they watched him.

Things went on like that for a while. Eventually Mr. Muscle announced in a solemn voice, "I've got it!"

"What? Well? Tell us! Go on! What will it be?" everyone burst out.

He took a sip of wine and said, "Rex!" He took another sip and asked, "What d'you think?"

There was a round of applause. "Perfect! Excellent! Very original! Bravo!"

Mr. Muscle looked at Plum with great pride. But, as he was opening his mouth to ask her if she liked Rex,

Plum declared, quite simply, "No." And Dog let out a sigh of relief.

"No? Why ever not?" asked Mrs. Squeak, hoping to avoid an argument.

"Because Rex isn't a name for real dogs; it's a name you give to dogs in books. And anyway, everyone calls their dog Rex. That's why not. And no means no."

There was an awkward silence, punctuated by the clinking of washing up.

Someone suggested, "What about Lassie then?"

"No," answered Plum, "I don't like Lassie either — it's the name of a dog in a movie."

Silence again. People were starting to realize that finding a name wasn't going to be so easy after all. A cloud seemed to settle over the table. Particularly over Mr. Muscle's head. A black cloud that threatened to spark flashes of lightning. Which is why everybody began to chip in.

"Buster!"

"Prince?"

"Ruffles!"

"Pluto? Fido? Sultan? Lancelot? Baron? Tarquin? Hal?"

Each time, Plum gave the same reply. "No."

And sometimes she gave a reason. "Too ugly. Boring. Pretentious. So many dogs are called that these days."

Until the black cloud finally burst over Mr. Muscle's head.

"All right then! Why don't you come up with a name yourself if you're so smart? Go on, hurry up and find one! Nothing yet? Mmm? Getting there? We're waiting!"

"Dog," answered Plum, just like that.

"Dog? Yes . . . and . . . ? Dog WHAT? WHAT ARE YOU GOING TO CALL YOUR DOG?"

68

"My dog will be called Dog," Plum explained patiently.

"What d'you mean, dog?" asked Mr. Muscle, with his eyes popping out of his head. "Dog — that's not a name!"

"It's the nicest, simplest, most original name I can think of. I don't know of any dog called Dog." And then she added, "Apart from mine," with a look that meant the matter had been settled and there was no going back.

"But all dogs are called dog, my pet!" Mrs. Squeak laughed awkwardly. "Think about it! That's where you'll find them, under *D* in the dictionary!" And she glanced apologetically at the guests.

"I've thought about it. And my dog is going to be called Dog, with a capital *D*, *because* there's only one dog like him in the whole wide world."

"You can say that again," agreed Mr. Muscle, winking slyly at everybody. "Actually, I think you're quite right not giving him a name. He's probably far too stupid to answer to one anyway."

Plum didn't reply. She smiled, stood up, and said, "Good night, everyone."

Dog didn't know what else to do, so he stayed sitting on the chair, until Plum asked without even turning around, "Are you coming, Dog?"

69

Dog instantly rushed to her, as if he'd been called Dog all his life.

A Dog Who Throws Up

Then vacation came to an end. Mr. Muscle, Plum, and Mrs. Squeak had to go back to the city.

The journey wasn't much fun for Dog. It had some good moments, but there were also a few hiccups. Dog hadn't been in a car before (not counting the trips from the town to the campsite and back, which were short and straight). So it was the first time he had really *traveled*. Mr. Muscle insisted on taking the mountain road that wound along the coast, because he said it was more picturesque. Dog sat in the back, next to Plum.

With each bend of the road, Dog could feel his insides churning. All this traveling was making him feel sick. Plum turned as white as a sheet when she saw

Dog throwing up, and promptly started throwing up herself. When Mrs. Squeak heard Plum throwing up, it made her want to throw up too. She rushed to open her window so that she'd be sick outside. All these people throwing up put Mr. Muscle in such a bad mood that he took it out on the other drivers. He seemed to think he was the only person who knew how to drive. He put his foot down on the accelerator and the car shot off, with the trailer wobbling behind.

Dog, who'd just managed to stick his nose out of the window, was in seventh heaven. All the smells in the world were spinning around inside his nose, like a **71** hurricane of treats. (He was starting to get the hang of all these bends in the road; he was even coming around to the idea that the car was one of human beings' better inventions.)

Sometimes they stopped for a drink, to fill up with gas, or to let the engine cool down. Occasionally Mr. Muscle would come across one of the drivers he'd criticized on the road. Dog was fascinated by these encounters. As he approached the driver, Mr. Muscle would flex his muscles and make himself look as intimidating as possible. The driver would flex his muscles too, if he was the same size as Mr. Muscle. And they would strike up a conversation. Dog had seen it all before at the dump. Two hefty dogs would approach each other, growling and making the fur on their muscular shoulders stand on end. Dog was convinced they'd massacre each other when he heard them snarling, heads held high, ears pressed back, and fangs glinting in the sunlight.

"And to think" — Black Nose used to smile without looking at them — "they're not even going to lay a paw on each other. It's all for show."

Sure enough, after sniffing around each other two or three times, each dog would retreat to his own territory and proudly cock a leg over the first tire he could find, as if he'd just won a great victory.

These men were just the same. They looked each other up and down and clenched their fists and snarled. You could see their gold fillings when they sneered. From time to time they shot glances at their fans (Plum and Mrs. Squeak were on the hood of the car, rooting for Mr. Muscle; another Plum and another Mrs. Squeak showed their support for the other driver). But they ended up going their own ways without coming to blows. Each man locked himself inside a special sort of cubicle, where Dog imagined he proudly cocked his leg. And the audience looked happy with the show.

Then came the highway, which seemed to go on forever. They drove . . . and they drove . . . and they drove. Dog would never have imagined you could cover so much road just getting from one place to another.

The highway bypassed plenty of towns, but it still cut through all their smells. Town after town flashed past. Plum and Mrs. Squeak were asleep. Mr. Muscle kept quiet.

Dog was being taken farther and farther away. He'd always lived in the same place, and he was starting to feel homesick. He was being separated from his puppyhood. Memories that kept drifting back made him feel even more unhappy: Black Nose under the fridge door, Woolly telling him to be brave when the going gets tough . . .

The sun was setting. They passed the body of a dog on the hard shoulder. It had been run over. Dodging, thought Dog, no knack for dodging. . . . The tears welled up inside him and popped like bubbles of sadness in the silent car.

My Dog? What Dog?

It was in the city that Plum and Dog's relationship started to go wrong. Up until then Plum had behaved perfectly. In fact, she'd been so kind, Dog thought she was already fully trained. She must have had a dog before, he told himself, one who really knew how to train her.

But Plum had never had a pet before, as Dog realized the moment he set his paws inside the apartment. No dog had ever lived there. And no cat or bird either, for that matter: they would have left a scent. The flat smelled of human beings and nothing else. It didn't take Dog long to figure out that Plum had acted on a whim when she came to the dog pound. Now that she was back home again, she was busy with her bedroom and her toys and her friends and her old routine. She'd forgotten all about Dog.

If the apartment had been a proper house with a garden, it wouldn't have mattered so much. Dog could have stayed outside all day long. He didn't need much to entertain him: a few birds, a gust of wind scattering the leaves, two or three suspicious noises to bark at, the odd trail to sniff out . . . and the time would soon fly by. But city apartments don't have gardens. Everybody lives indoors, and indoors is no fun at all. It's small, for a start. And it's even smaller for a dog than it is for a person, because of all the places that are out of bounds. Dog's not allowed on the sofa or armchairs, he's not allowed to lie on the living room carpet (which takes up the whole of the living room), and he's not allowed in Mr. Muscle and Mrs. Squeak's bedroom. . . . All that's left is the entryway (two square yards), the tiny kitchen (when Mrs. Squeak isn't cooking), the hallway (where everyone trips over him), and Plum's bedroom (but not at night).

Except that Plum didn't want Dog in her bedroom.

"Can't you let me play in peace? Go and find your own space."

Dog moved to the hall. He sighed as he lay down in front of Plum's closed door.

Mrs. Squeak chose precisely that moment to come out of her bedroom. She tripped over Dog and started shouting. "That stupid dog's always getting in my way! Can't you go and find somewhere else to lie down?"

Head down, Dog moved off to hide under the kitchen table. He stayed there until lunchtime, when Mrs. Squeak chased him out again.

"I'm not having a dog in my kitchen when I'm getting a meal ready. It's unhygienic!" ("Hygienic" and "unhygienic" were words that kept popping up in Mrs. Squeak's vocabulary. Dog was mostly *un*hygienic.)

So he got up, left the kitchen to hide in the entryway, and whimpered as he rolled himself into a ball under the coat rack. But the front door suddenly opened: Mr. Muscle was back from work. He hung his coat on the peg. Two gallons of rainwater poured onto Dog's back. The shower took him by surprise, so Dog ran into the living room, where he shook himself like a duck after a diving session. This made a fan of shiny droplets and triggered a big argument.

"My living room!" shrieked Mrs. Squeak in a horrified tone. She was in the dining room, setting the table. Her eyes flashed. She pointed a finger that shook with fury at Mr. Muscle. "You've soaked that animal again with your raincoat! How many times do I have to remind you to shake it off outside?"

"And how many times do I have to tell you the entry is no place for a dog?" replied Mr. Muscle in his voice that boomed like brass.

"*Excuse me*, but who wanted Dog in the first place? You know I've always been against the idea."

"Look who's talking! If I'd paid any attention to you, there'd be an enormous woolly sheepdog sprawled across our doorstep. We wouldn't even be able to get the door open!" sneered Mr. Muscle.

"If you'd listened to me, we wouldn't have a dog at all! You're the one who gave in to your little princess, as usual."

"D'you think you two could stop arguing?" suggested a third voice. "I can't read with all this noise, and you're setting a very bad example for my dolls."

"Perfect timing! How about looking after *your* dog for once? Hmm?"

Mr. Muscle and Mrs. Squeak suddenly joined forces against Plum, who was leaning against the living room door and staring defiantly at them with a book in her hand. Caught in the crossfire, Dog didn't know what to think. Mr. Muscle and Mrs. Squeak frightened him;

Plum made him sad. And on this particular day she hurt him more than ever. When the grownups asked "How about looking after *your* dog for once?" her reply was unbelievable. She looked curiously around the living room, as if trying to find something, and she took a good look around the dining room too before glancing into the entryway and kitchen. Then she answered with a wide-eyed stare, "What dog?"

And she went back to her room.

Self-Respect

Things went on like that for some time. And it was torture for Dog.

In the mornings Plum went to school and Mr. Muscle went to work. Mrs. Squeak stayed in the apartment on her own. It made Dog feel even lonelier having her around. Mrs. Squeak took care of everything in the house except him. When she'd finished cleaning her bedroom, she tidied up Plum's bedroom. Next she dusted in the living room and did all the vacuuming before attacking the windows and polishing the knickknacks so they reflected the inside of the apartment like funny-shaped mirrors. And then she went into the kitchen to get lunch ready.

All this was done as if Dog didn't exist. In fact, Dog started to wonder if he really *did* exist. So, toward the end of those awful mornings, he began to bark for no reason. He just wanted to hear the sound of his own voice.

"What's the matter with you? Are you going crazy?" shrieked Mrs. Squeak, looking like a Greek Fury as she bustled out of the kitchen. "Be quiet! What *will* the neighbors think?"

Dog felt reassured: yes, he really *did* exist.

At midday, when her daughter and husband came home, Mrs. Squeak always greeted them with the same news. "Dog's spent the whole morning barking!"

And Mr. Muscle always asked the same question. "Why didn't you take him out for a walk?"

Mrs. Squeak would look aghast. "Take him out for a walk? As if I haven't got enough to do!"

And Mr. Muscle would always come to the same conclusion. "That's why he's barking. He wants to go out." Then he would turn to his daughter and add, "You should start taking YOUR dog for a walk before lunch."

"Can't," Plum always answered back. "Got to get my school bag ready for this afternoon."

Before Mr. Muscle could say another word, Plum would shut herself in her bedroom, and Mrs. Squeak would shut herself in her kitchen. And Mr. Muscle would find himself alone with Dog. He'd peer down, his upper lip curled with distaste. "All right, I suppose *I've* got to do it."

From the coat rack he'd take a leash strong enough to tether a bull, clip it to Dog's collar, and head out into the street, grumbling, "Be quick about it!"

But dogs are never quick when it comes to these kinds of things. It takes at least ten tires before they find one with the right kind of smell. And then they have to sniff it for a long time, to be sure about what kind of dog they're dealing with. Only after this detailed examination are they ready to cock a leg. But even then they have to hold back reserve supplies for any other smells that might be as inviting as the first. It's a question of principle, and dogs always honor it. Black Nose was very strict on this matter. "We're a large family," she would say, "and don't ever forget it."

But Mr. Muscle wasn't the slightest bit interested in any of this. Dog had barely inspected the first tire when Mr. Muscle began tugging on the leash. Dog dug in his heels with all his strength. Mr. Muscle waited for a second or so. And then he felt so ridiculous in front of the other passersby that he gave a big tug. Dog came unstuck, leaving a trail of droplets in the air. And they went back home.

And that was that.

"I'll never understand why dogs have to pee on *every* car tire they go past!" thundered Mr. Muscle as he sat down to lunch.

The apartment was empty until five o'clock in the afternoon. Plum went back to school and Mr. Muscle went back to work. Mrs. Squeak went window-shopping. Dog stayed by himself. It was better like that. At least he wasn't getting in anyone's way. And the silence allowed him to think. So he reflected on things. Mr. Muscle's and Mrs. Squeak's behavior wasn't surprising, because they'd never loved him anyway. But Plum? *Plum?*

How could she have loved him and then stopped loving him, out of the blue? What had he done to make her behave so differently? Nothing. She was a strange owner. And human beings were so unpredictable.

Dog was upset, of course. But he also felt ashamed and angry. The truth was, he hadn't been able to train Plum properly. Black Nose would have been furious with him. She hadn't sent him to town just to find an owner; she'd also expected him to train her. And he'd failed miserably. He'd let himself be coddled like a spoiled child as long as Plum's whim had lasted. And now that she'd lost interest in him, he didn't know what to do anymore. How do you train someone who doesn't even see you? All these ideas went around in his head until he didn't know what to think. At times like this, when he felt completely lost, he remembered what Woolly had said about the mistress who'd abandoned him.

"What good would it have done following her? If she didn't want me anymore, what was the point?"

And then Sniffy had spoken about self-respect. Self-respect. . . . Dog was beginning to have an inkling of what self-respect might be.

Plum had abandoned him, just like Woolly's mistress. That was the truth. And Dog was hanging on, waiting. For what? For Plum's love to blossom again? Not likely. Weren't his creature comforts and daily food the only things keeping him here? His self-respect was in a sorry state. And to think he'd been embarrassed by Sniffy's behavior in front of the journalists. . . . How was he any better than Sniffy, staying in an apartment where Plum pretended he didn't exist, Mrs. Squeak complained about having him around, and Mr. Muscle took him out on a leash as if he were a kite?

When you reflect on things, you reach certain conclusions.

When you reach certain conclusions, you make a decision.

When you make a decision, you have to act on it.

Dog decided to escape.

And he did.

The Great Escape

That's right. He escaped from Plum's apartment. You'd never believe it if you could see him now, sleeping soundly in the little girl's bed without a dream in his head. You'd never think that, for a while, Plum had actually stopped loving him.

Plum is sitting on the bed, propped up on her pillow. She's wrapped a scarf around her bedside lamp because she doesn't want to wake Dog. She turns the pages of her book as quietly as she can.

All of a sudden she stops reading and strokes him gently. He lets out a long, happy sigh in his sleep. Plum starts reading again.

And to think that not so long ago he ran away. You'd never believe it!

☆   ☆   ☆

It happened on a Thursday . . . or a Friday. Everyone had gone out. Mrs. Squeak had left the kitchen window ajar to air the place. (She complained that the apartment smelled of Dog.)

Cautiously Dog poked his head outside. Then he squeezed his whole body through the gap and sat down on Mrs. Squeak's window box. Instantly he noticed the smell of autumn in the air. It was a heavy, russet-colored smell that rose skyward. While he was sitting comfortably on the compost, Dog was having second thoughts. When there's such a strong smell of autumn, he thought, it means there's a hard winter ahead. An icy shiver ran down his spine. Below the window was the caretaker's roof. And underneath that was the shed. And next to the shed was the door to the courtyard. It was wide open. (There'd just been a fuel delivery. Everyone was getting ready for winter.) The evening was settling in. Mrs. Squeak would be back any moment. And Dog was still having second thoughts.

"Don't wait too long," whispered Black Nose's voice inside him. "Hesitation is a dog's worst enemy."

"And what about your self-respect?" came another voice, Woolly's this time.

"I know," answered Dog, "but this city is so huge, it

frightens me, and I don't have any friends out there, and it's going to be freezing cold this winter!"

Then Dog recognized a third voice sniffily asking, "You silly sausage, which would you prefer? Stay inside in the warm, where they'll boss you around with a broom handle? Or run about free in the cold? A dog is an independent animal, my friend, in-de-pen-dent!"

These voices might have gone on for a very long time inside Dog's head if they hadn't been interrupted by another voice that was unmistakably real and coming from the middle of the courtyard.

Mrs. Squeak was shouting with her hands on her hips. "What are you doing on the window box? How dare you sit on my plants! Just you wait till I get my hands on you!"

Dog didn't hang around. While Mrs. Squeak was racing up the stairs, three at a time, he jumped down onto the caretaker's roof, down onto the shed roof, and found himself outside.

Outside. All alone. In the city.

Dog started running, the way dogs run when they've escaped. He ran and he ran and he ran. He'd made up his mind he was never coming back. He even tried holding his breath to lose track of his own scent. But running and holding your breath is a tiring combination. Dog ended up collapsing next to a colorful newspaper stand, completely winded.

What should he do now? Find another mistress? No, thank you. This one had caused him enough pain. What, then? He remembered the butcher from the town. He even tried sniffing out that lavender smell, but it was hopeless. What good is a sensitive nose when there are hundreds of miles between you and the smell? And then he noticed just how big the city was. It seemed to spread out forever, from the gas fumes close by all the way to the factory smoke on the horizon. Was it a city at all? Or had the whole world been covered with buildings overnight?

Dog panicked. I have to get out, he told himself, right away. It doesn't matter how. I just need to find another dump, get back to my old way of life, find some other dogs, find a place where I don't feel so alone, so lost.

Night had crept up on Dog while these thoughts were flying around inside his head. And something strange was happening. The newspaper stand next to him had disappeared behind its wooden shutters. This was the signal for streetlights to be switched on, windows to light up, and buildings to empty people onto the sidewalks. Out they trooped by the thousands, from every direction. Store blinds were lowered, office doors slammed, and keys turned in locks. Cars rushed out of the small side streets to pile into the main road, where the traffic in front of Dog's eyes inched forward as slowly as a glacier.

Some people headed off silently and alone. Others formed small groups and spoke in lowered voices. Then the loners and the groups joined to make a crowd. But the crowd disappeared slowly underground, swallowed by a big black hole in the brightly lit road.

Dog cheered up when he saw this spectacle. Perhaps, like him, these people were trying to leave the city. He imagined they'd dug underground tunnels for their escape route (that's what the rats used to do underneath the dump), and he decided to follow them. So he caught up with the crowd and made his way underground. Down long corridors of shiny ceramic tiles that made the footsteps ring in his ears, until he found himself on a platform. It seemed to be a sort of railway platform, because a kind of train pulled up with a screeching of brakes. That's what it must be, thought Dog, who'd seen trains going past, high above the dump. As soon as a door opened, he jumped into the subway car with a pounding heart. Instinctively he lay down under a seat so it would look like he belonged to someone. (Better safe than sorry, since he was the only dog in this sea of humans.) There was a beeping noise, the doors slid shut, and the train moved off.

The train kept stopping all the time. At some stations it all but emptied itself. So Dog followed the biggest crowd in the greatest hurry. He expected to come out somewhere in the middle of the countryside. But the crowd never seemed to get to the surface. It went back down more tile tunnels, pushed its way onto more platforms, and scrambled on board more trains, only to clamber back out again and follow mile after mile of underground passageways.

Dog ran as fast as his short legs would carry him, between countless pairs of shoes that seemed to be getting louder and quicker all the time. Another train pulled up, and the door slid shut. They must have left the city far behind. The passengers were thinning out now. They seemed exhausted by the long journey. But they kept running faster and faster when they changed trains.

Eventually Dog found himself alone in a subway car with a man who was also alone and too tired to notice him. When this last passenger got out, Dog followed, hoping the man would at least lead him back up to ground level. And, sure enough, the passenger headed up. Slowly, step by step, they climbed a staircase littered with blue tickets and cigarette stubs. The black night sky appeared at last above their heads. Dog was so happy, he let out a victory bark as he took three leaps and found himself outside.

What Dog felt next doesn't bear describing. He was so paralyzed with shock that he landed with a bump and didn't move for a very long time. All around him the fronts of huge, sleepy buildings rose up. But they weren't any old buildings. They were exactly the same as the ones he'd been looking at when he'd decided to follow the crowd down into the big black hole. He recognized the newspaper stand behind its wooden shutters, the stores with their closed blinds, the dark windows of empty offices. He'd arrived back at exactly the same spot! The side streets and the main road were as brightly lit as before. But they were deserted now.

Dog sat still as a stone and howled and howled

without drawing breath, eyes closed, neck strained, and mouth wide open. . . .

He'd probably still be shouting today if a voice hadn't suddenly whispered in his ear, "What's going on? D'you want to wake the whole neighborhood?"

Hyena

Dog jumped out of his skin, landed on his feet, bared his teeth, and bristled from head to tail. There, standing before him, was the most terrifying vision he'd ever seen. Two yellow eyes stared back at him above a strong black mouth with two fangs as deadly as butcher's hooks. A great tuft of fur sprouted from the top of the creature's head. It was a dirty yellow color streaked with black, like the fur of a wild animal. But most striking of all was the way the two front legs (which were much longer and more muscular than the back legs) framed an enormous chest. The creature was three or four times the size of Dog, and it didn't move. Dog didn't move either. He just growled and bristled, ready to fight for his life. He remembered seeing an animal a bit like this once before. One day, when Plum had a book open on her lap, she'd shown him a picture.

"Take a look at that. It's a hyena. Don't you think he looks horrible?" she'd asked in a voice full of awe.

And he'd certainly looked horrible enough. But that kind of vision is much less frightening in a picture than when it's suddenly standing in front of you in the middle of the night in the big city.

Could the vision read Dog's thoughts? It burst into an icy peal of laughter and declared, "I know I'm no oil painting. I look like a hyena. And don't tell me I don't, because I know I do. Everyone calls me Hyena. But then you're no beauty yourself, you know."

Hyena started laughing again, and he sounded like a chuckling waterfall. ("Apparently hyenas giggle all the time," Plum had told Dog.)

"Why don't you tell me what's wrong, instead of trembling like a leaf and baring those tiny teeth of yours?" suggested Hyena, who'd suddenly stopped laughing.

The funny thing was that when Hyena spoke, his voice was very soft and gentle. Dog wasn't sure if he found this reassuring or alarming. After a great effort, he eventually managed to say, "I'm lost."

"Not anymore," said Hyena. "I know this city like the back of my hand. Where d'you want to go?"

"The thing is, I want to get out of the city," said Dog, trying to sound a bit more confident.

"And go where?" asked Hyena, without taking his eyes off him.

"I don't know . . . south, maybe," answered Dog, looking into those phosphorescent eyes.

"Fine. I've got to be at the station for the twelve minutes past midnight. Follow me," ordered Hyena. And without waiting for an answer, he turned and headed off down the road.

At first Dog followed at a respectful distance. Hyena had a strange way of walking. Those impressive shoulders thrust his front legs out proudly, while his back legs trailed behind. From time to time he knocked over a garbage can carelessly with his nose and asked without looking back, "Are you hungry?"

Gradually Dog started catching up with Hyena. Soon he was trotting alongside him. Dog felt as proud as if he'd just tamed a lion or a tiger. And he began spilling his story, even though Hyena hadn't asked him to. He talked without drawing breath, like you do when you want to get everything off your chest.

Hyena knitted his eyebrows together as he listened. They were black and shiny, like a tiger's bristles. From time to time he would ask a question.

"So this man you call Mr. Muscle never let you spray tires?"

"Never."

"That doesn't surprise me."

"Why not?"

"I'll tell you later. Go on."

So Dog went on. He didn't tell his story in the right order. Like anyone who's feeling upset, he kept coming back to the same thing: Plum's strange behavior.

"She forgot about you just like that, from one day to the next?" asked Hyena.

"Yes, without any warning."

"That doesn't surprise me," Hyena said again.

"Why not?" asked Dog, coming to a halt.

"I'll tell you later. Don't stop. I'm in a hurry."

They kept on walking, down brightly lit roads that had led to shadowy side streets, and down shadowy side streets that fed into dark passages, until eventually they reached the train station. There, great black buildings rose up like silent giants. Dog couldn't see a thing — except for Hyena's eyes glowing right next to him. Everything smelled of tar, damp, and rust.

"A bit grim, hey?" whispered Hyena in his strange reedy voice. And, as if he wanted to scare Dog even more, he let out a peal of laughter that kept bouncing back off the maze of walls in the depot.

Finally they climbed a mound of gravel that slipped beneath their weight. When they reached the top, Dog felt something icy under his paws. High in the sky there was a break in the cloud. For a fraction of a second Dog could see rail tracks gleaming as far as the horizon.

"There you go," said Hyena. "South is that way, straight ahead. Nice meeting you."

And he disappeared.

The clouds closed over again. Dog would never have believed a night could be so dark. He couldn't even see his own paws. He couldn't have been there longer than a few seconds, but he was so terrified it seemed like hours.

Then, unable to contain himself any longer, he cried out, "Hyena! Hyena! Don't leave me here. . . ."

There was no answer. Just the night. And a gust of wind full of dark smells.

"Hyena! *Please!* " There were tears in Dog's voice.

Far off in the distance, Hyena's laugh answered him. One moment it sounded far away, and the next it was close by. Then it was far away. Then close again. The sound of his laughter filled the air.

"Stop frightening me!" Dog suddenly exploded. "Stop it at once! Or else —"

"Or else what?" asked a disturbingly kind voice right beside him.

Before Dog could answer, a heavy blow sent him rolling down into the ditch below the platform. He felt very dizzy as he tried to pick himself up, but two yellow eyes nailed him to the spot.

"So you don't want to head south anymore?" And there was a fresh peal of laughter. Then, still laughing, Hyena ordered, "Come on — follow me. We're going to find Wild Boar."

Hyena and Wild Boar

There are lots of things you could say about Hyena, because he was a complex character. He loved practical jokes, for a start. He tried them out at every opportunity, and they weren't always in the best taste. But no one ever got angry with him because Hyena was very popular. Actually, it irritated him that everyone was so fond of him — he wanted to be known as a cruel, wild beast.

"With a face like mine I deserve a bit of respect, don't you think?"

Hyena's problem was that he was too kind for his own good. The moment he'd heard Dog crying, he'd decided to look after him. It was in his nature to help out and fight injustice and try to understand everyone's point of view.

"Trouble is," he said, "I'm allergic to biting. . . ." And a confused smile spread across his face, revealing two enormous fangs that were yellow and slightly worn at the tips because he wasn't a young dog anymore.

"But if someone attacked Wild Boar, would you defend him?" Dog asked him.

The look on Hyena's face changed immediately, and Dog felt the same terror that had run through him on the evening of their first encounter.

"There's only one Wild Boar, and no one messes with him!" Then the smile returned to his lips, and he added, "No one messes with my friends."

Wild Boar was a ticket inspector, or an engine driver, or something like that. A railway man, at any rate. That was his job.

When he saw the two dogs waiting for him to arrive on the twelve minutes past midnight, he said casually, "Hello, Hyena. So you've brought a friend with you? Well, he's certainly not a looker. Nature excelling herself again!"

Hyena split his sides with laughter, and all three of them soon found themselves in Wild Boar's home.

When he took his cap off, Wild Boar really *was* the spitting image of a wild boar. He had a big head with stiff eyebrows and black hair he couldn't pull a comb through. He was very solid, and not a pretty picture. "When we catch the subway together," said Hyena, "everyone leaves the car."

Wild Boar's apartment was a cross between a treasure trove and a junk shop. There were paintings all over the walls, and everywhere you looked statues patiently carved out of heavy wood by Wild Boar. Some of these works of art depicted Hyena himself. But they showed a very handsome Hyena — the sort of Hyena he might have been in real life, if real life hadn't botched the job. What was striking about Wild Boar's work was the way he'd managed to catch Hyena's intelligence, not to mention his bravery and recklessness, as well as his taste for practical jokes. But, underneath all of that, he'd also caught the serious side of his character — a distant sadness that couldn't be seen with the naked eye or in a photograph. Those pictures and sculptures bore more than a passing resemblance. Hanging from the walls and proudly positioned over the mantelpiece, they really did look like him.

Dog immediately recognized Hyena. "Well I never! It's you! How d'you manage to look so handsome up there?"

"Love changes the way you see things. . . ." Hyena answered, trying to look modest.

And so Dog moved in with Hyena and Wild Boar. The apartment was both of theirs because you couldn't really say it just belonged to Wild Boar. Hyena had exactly the same rights as his owner (although he always referred to him as his friend rather than his owner) and none of the rooms were out of bounds. But Hyena didn't try to take advantage of this.

"I don't sleep in his bed. We're both so big we'd get in each other's way."

Every other day Hyena and Dog would accompany Wild Boar to the station. Sometimes it was a morning trip, and sometimes an evening one. Then they would take a stroll together through the streets of the city.

Seduction Is the Only Answer

After their stroll they'd head back to Wild Boar's apartment. Hyena knew how to open all the doors, which is no mean feat for a dog. He also knew how to close them again, which is even more impressive.

"You need to learn these tricks if you want to keep your independence: shutting a door, wiping your paws, drinking from the tap. . . ."

"But who taught you?" asked Dog.

"Wild Boar, of course."

Dog didn't understand how Wild Boar could be Hyena's owner and teach him to be a free dog at the same time.

"He's not my owner," repeated Hyena for the umpteenth time. "He's my friend!"

"What's the difference between an owner and a friend?" asked Dog.

Hyena patiently explained.

He taught Dog everything. Everything Black Nose hadn't had time to teach him. Everything Woolly would have taught him if they hadn't met at the dog pound.

"Thanks to those two, you already know a great deal," pointed out Hyena, who was clearly impressed. "Because of Black Nose you've got the best nose for smells of any dog I've met, you can pick out choice cuts at first glance, and there's no danger of you being run over by a car. As for your friend from the dog pound, didn't he teach you about bravery and loyalty? They were both fine dogs. You were lucky to have met them."

Dog agreed. And now Hyena was filling in the gaps. He spoke to Dog about human beings, about human beings and dogs, and about the relationships between them.

"What d'you do if a human being wants to hit you, for example?"

"I attack him first!" replied Dog, bristling.

"You nitwit! You couldn't frighten a fly!"

"That's not true!" protested Dog. "I frightened a fat lady in the town."

"I know — you told me. But only because she was shortsighted and mistook you for a rat. Human beings are scared stiff of rats."

"All right then, what am I supposed to do if a human being attacks me?"

"You sit back, make yourself look as idiotic as possible and stare, tilting your head to the side, with one ear drooping and the other pricked up."

"And where does that get you?"

"It makes them go all gooey, simple as that. You won't find a human who doesn't become as gentle as a lamb after that, however tough they think they are."

Hyena looked thoughtful all of a sudden. "I'm going to tell you something very important, Dog." He was concentrating so hard that his whole forehead crumpled up.

"Yes?"

"Here goes. . . . When you're as ugly as we are, seduction is the only answer."

"What does *seduction* mean?"

Hyena's whole head disappeared into the furrows on his brow.

"It means knowing how to make people *want* you."

"And how d'you do that?"

Silence. Followed by a long stare, and then a sigh.

"I'll teach you that too."

Mixed-Up Kids

Dog talked about Plum all the time. He described every aspect of her character: how stubborn she was, the tantrums she flew into, how kind and gentle she'd been those first few days, the power she had over grownups, her unexpected cruelty later on, everything.

"I don't want to disappoint you," yawned Hyena, "but your little Plum isn't unusual. She's just a kid like all the rest. She's getting ready to become a grownup, but for the time being she's all mixed up."

"Mixed up?"

"Well . . . fickle, if you prefer. That's what adults call it. But she's not really fickle. She's just mixed up, because she doesn't really know what she wants yet."

Dog didn't understand, so Hyena took him to see other mixed-up kids. It was a gray afternoon, except for a tiny ray of sunlight between three and four o'clock. School playgrounds and parks were filled with tiny, noisy children making the most of the sunshine. Dog and Hyena sat next to each other on the other side of the railings, watching.

The children were playing (if you could call it playing) under the chestnut trees. Are those really games? Dog wondered. The children were taking part in complicated activities in pairs or small groups. One moment they were as quiet as mice, and the next a fight would break out. But then the arguments stopped as suddenly as they began, and everyone went back to playing.

108

In a corner of the playground near the slide, Dog noticed a short fat boy with a bright pink face. He was sitting on his bottom and bawling his eyes out. His mouth was open wide and the tears splashed down his cheeks. He looks so sad he might die, thought Dog, who felt faint. But a chestnut leaf twirled in the air and landed just in front of the short fat pink creature. He stopped crying, just like that, and smiled angelically at the leaf, as if nothing else mattered in the world.

A little girl on the path was saying something to another little girl, who was all ears. A third little girl wandered past. The little girl who'd been listening left the little girl who'd been talking to catch up with the little girl who'd wandered past. The little girl who'd been talking carried on talking to herself, giggling at the end of every sentence as if nothing had happened. She walked past the sand, and there Dog noticed Tidy Boy.

Tidy Boy had a bucket and spade and he'd just built a fourteenth tower for his sandcastle. It was a beautiful tower with crenelations, machicolations, and arrow slits. Tidy Boy wore glasses and he was concentrating very hard. He'd traced the outlines of stone blocks on a series of ramparts linking his towers. Right now he was polishing the surface of the fourteenth tower with the back of his spade, carefully blowing away the excess sand and feasting his eyes on his handiwork. How long had it taken him to build? He must have the patience of a saint, thought Dog.

Tidy Boy lifted his head. There was a strange glint in his eye. He jumped up, stretched out his arms, and began making an engine noise, circling his castle like a motorized bird. Then, without warning: "TA-TA-

TA-TA-TA-TA-TA-BANG!" He kicked over towers and ramparts; there were explosions, showers of sand, clouds of dust, and ugly craters. What a disaster! Soon nothing was left of the magnificent sandcastle and its fourteen towers. Then, just like that, Tidy Boy stopped being a fighter-bomber. He picked up his spade, stowed it neatly in his bucket, and headed off as if nothing had happened.

Silence. The first drops of rain began to fall.

Dog was flabbergasted.

"Now do you understand?" Hyena asked at last.

But Dog couldn't answer. He just stayed where he was. Hyena's right, he thought. These kids are just as mixed up as Plum. They change games and interests and the looks on their faces faster than the wind changes direction. And they're just as unpredictable. They're never the same, from one moment to the next.

And Dog remembered the days (which already seemed a long time ago) when he couldn't manage to follow one smell at a time. He'd been just as mixed up as these kids. Now, for the first time, he understood what Hyena meant when he said, "We grow up seven times faster than they do, and that's what makes it difficult."

Without even realizing it, Dog had become an adult. But Plum was still a child. And she was all mixed up, the way kids are.

It was raining buckets. And the playground was empty. Dog was lost in his daydreams, but he could just make out the far-off sound of Hyena's voice.

"Come on — follow me. We're going to find Wild Boar."

Too Good to Be True

Hyena never made a mistake when it came to train timetables. He had a sixth sense. Wild Boar always found Dog and Hyena waiting at the end of platform six. And all three of them would head home, happy to be together.

In fact, they were *so* happy, Dog began to wonder if it wasn't too good to be true. It worried him. It was too perfect to last. Not that Wild Boar and Hyena had any such doubts. They seemed to think it was perfectly normal to be happy. Dog watched them carefully. Because they'd grown so used to each other, they didn't need to show their affection anymore. Not much, anyway. Hyena would discreetly wag his tail when

Wild Boar arrived, and Wild Boar would vaguely stroke Hyena's head before talking to him as naturally as if he were picking up the thread of an interrupted conversation.

The happier they were, the sadder Dog felt inside. How strange, he thought. Perhaps there's something wrong with me. But he couldn't shake off the feeling. He watched Wild Boar pick up his paintbrushes and look at Hyena out of the corner of his eye. While Wild Boar daubed the first colors onto a fresh canvas and Hyena found a flattering pose, horrible images floated across Dog's mind.

They were always the same: the fridge door spinning in the sky, Black Nose's body abandoned in the garbage, the dog-pound van, Woolly's last look, the corpse of that other dog on the hard shoulder of the highway. The same visions kept haunting him, and they made him feel ashamed. He didn't tell Hyena about it because he didn't want to spoil his happiness. But you couldn't hide anything from Hyena.

"What's the matter, Dog? You look worried!"

"Oh, it's nothing. I'm fine, really."

"Well, if you're sure . . ."

Hyena didn't probe any further. Experience had taught him that when Dog couldn't stand it anymore, he'd tell him the whole story.

Which is, of course, exactly what happened. One day Dog couldn't stand it anymore. He'd fallen asleep in that painfully happy atmosphere, and his nightmares had come back to haunt him. He woke up yelping so loudly that Wild Boar squished three tubes of paint in his huge hands and Hyena bristled like a pincushion.

"Hey . . . hey . . . what's going on? What's the matter, Dog? Tell us! Say something, for goodness' sake!"

"The thing is . . ." panted Dog. "The thing is . . . I'm too happy here with you. It feels like a dream. Real life isn't like this. It's something else, something completely different. It's full of run-over dogs on the hard shoulders of highways, and dead dogs abandoned among the rubbish. It's full of black vans, and dog-pound directors with blank smiles, and fridges that squash us, and owners who desert us. It's full of puppies who get drowned because they're too ugly. That's what real life's like. . . .

"The thing is . . . the thing is . . . I keep thinking you're both a dream. And so I worry I'm going to wake up on the highway, or at the bottom of a garbage dump, and I'll die there, all alone, like a dog. I'll die like all dogs die, abandoned by their owners. Because there's no such thing as friends; it's all a pack of lies. Owners are the only people who exist. Owners who think we're stupid and ugly and a nuisance when we take too much time sniffing smells. Who strangle us with their leashes and squash us with their cars. Who abandon our corpses and leave us all alone while the cars just keep on driving past. . . ."

And so on, in a never-ending lament. It was a cry for help from far back in the history of dogs — a cry that could have risen up in the throat of any miserable dog on a sad evening.

Wild Boar stood there, his enormous hands caked in paint that was oozing down onto the carpet. He kept looking furtively at Hyena, as if to say, "Come on then, *do* something, for heaven's sake!" But there was nothing Hyena could do except wait.

When Dog had no more breath left in him and he'd emptied his bag of unhappiness, he just stood there. His heart was pounding, his legs were buckling, his throat was dry, and the tip of his nose was on fire.

Hyena waited until Dog was completely numb and

helpless, and then he said to him, "Follow me, Dog. I want to show you something. And you can tell me if it's a dream."

He spoke with so much authority that it had the effect of a cold shower on Dog. Hyena had already opened the front door and was waiting outside on the landing. Dog followed him without a word.

The Dogs' Cemetery

They crossed the city. Night had long since fallen. At one stage in the journey Hyena ordered, "Wait here for me."

Dog sat down and waited, but not for long. Hyena reappeared around the street corner, carrying a large bird in his mouth and running flat out. A fat man in a white apron was running after him and shouting "Stop, thief!" in a rasping voice. Passersby laughed. Hyena swept in front of Dog's nose like a whirlwind. Dog paused for a split second before hurling himself at the pursuer's legs.

There was a great cry, followed by a sound like a jumbo jet making a crash landing, and the night sky spun underneath them. Dog bounced back onto the pavement. Without pausing to think, and still feeling very dazed, he ran after Hyena, who'd just disappeared around the other corner.

Once he'd caught up, Dog started asking a whole heap of questions. He was very excited. "Where are we going? What are you going to do with that bird? D'you think the man in the white apron is dead? Are you listening to me? *Where are we going?*"

But Hyena was walking in stealthy silence, his jaws clamped on his prey and the sparkle in his eye even brighter than usual.

Finally they reached the river. They were on the outskirts of the city. Factories rose up behind the yellowish curtain of light from the old streetlamps. Water flowed past, black as the sky above it. A garishly lit bridge cut through the darkness with a dazzling shaft of light. Hyena seemed to hesitate for a moment. He frowned and his pupils narrowed to the size of pinheads. He was looking in the direction of the light shaft. Dog watched him.

All of a sudden Hyena's eyes fixed on something. Dog followed his gaze. And then, for the first time, Dog saw it. Over there, at the other end of the bridge, a dark mass of trees rose up out of the river. They were gigantic trees. And, despite the rumbling from the city, Dog could hear their leaves rustling. They were shaking their foliage over a little island in midstream. Lit from underneath, their leaves sent out short silvery messages into the night.

Hyena continued his journey. Dog followed him up onto the bridge between the high walls of dazzling light. It was the first chance he'd had to get a proper look at the bird. What a set of feathers! He could see gold, and a red that was redder than he could ever have imagined, and dozens of other colors that were even brighter than Wild Boar's paints.

Dog started asking questions again. "What are you going to do with the bird? What breed is it? Are you listening to me? Are those feathers real or fake?"

Hyena still didn't answer. He walked with his head held high and his neck straining under the weight of the bird, which was even bigger than Dog.

Finally they reached the end of the bridge and stood in front of a stone archway. There was an inscription high up, but Dog couldn't read it. The cast-iron gate was wide open, beckoning visitors inside. But Hyena didn't go in. He took two steps forward, put the bird down between the two pillars of the archway, and then backed away to sit down and wait. Dog sat down next to him.

"Where are we?" he whispered.

"At the dogs' cemetery," Hyena replied, without any sign of emotion.

"What are we waiting for?" murmured Dog, who was torn between wanting to go inside and the impulse to scamper off.

"We're just waiting. You'll see."

It was dark beyond the archway. Cloaked in shadow, the cemetery looked empty. You could just make out a statue representing a St. Bernard, with a cask of rum around its neck and a child held tenderly in its enormous mouth. The wind sighed. Water splashed against the banks of the island.

Dog and Hyena had been waiting for some time when a cat suddenly appeared. It was a beautiful Egyptian cat, with a long, muscular, sand-colored body. She seemed to have been born out of the darkness. Dog jumped out of his skin and started to growl threateningly.

"Be quiet," ordered Hyena.

The cat sat down in front of Dog and Hyena and watched them without looking the slightest bit worried. In fact, she seemed completely at ease. She waited for Dog to calm down before picking up the bird by the neck and dragging it inside the cemetery. Then, and only then, did Hyena give the all clear.

"Let's go."

The cemetery wasn't as dark as it had looked from outside. Here and there, light from the bridge shone through the lower branches of the trees. It fell on the graves at oblique angles, like shafts of sunlight in a cathedral. But the dark night hemmed them in. There were all kinds of graves, from huge monuments to tiny square headstones. Some were made of marble, others of granite or concrete, and every sort of name was inscribed on them. In gold letters were names like Rex, Prince, Baron, and Tarquin. Carved out of stone or painted directly onto concrete were Buster, Lassie, Fido, Ruffles, and Lucky. Hyena read their names out respectfully, together with the loving words their owners had inscribed underneath.

"'To our friend Ruffles. You'll always be in our thoughts. . . .' 'To my dearest Hal, a trusty companion in good times and bad . . .' 'Farewell, Tarquin, my grief knows no bounds. . . .' 'Dearest Buster, a nobler character than I could ever be . . .'" And so on.

Between all the graves covered in flowers, tall strong trees had sprung up.

"They're not really trees," remarked Hyena. "They're dogs who've been changed into trees."

But what surprised Dog most was the number of cats roaming around the cemetery. You'd have thought it was *their* kingdom. One of them, a black cat who was slim and lithe and serene, was making a pretty picture with her claws in the sand surrounding a grave of pink porphyry decorated with feathers. Dog immediately recognized the feathers.

"That's right," said Hyena. "Human beings look after our cemetery and decorate it in the daytime, but it's the cats who take over at night. And a very good job they do too!" he added, nodding toward a pair of yellow eyes not far off, staring unblinkingly out of the darkness.

There was a flowery grave immediately to the right of the cemetery gate. It belonged to a dog without an owner who'd decided to sleep at last in the Cemetery of Happy Dogs.

Dog wanted to take another look around. Hyena agreed. Dog wanted Hyena to read out the names carved on the gravestones again. Hyena did a roll call of all the dogs in the cemetery. Dog wanted to hear the epitaphs again. Hyena read them out. Dog wanted to go around a third time. Hyena refused.

"No," he said, "we've got to get back."

They headed toward the exit in silence.

Human beings are so unpredictable, thought Dog (or something like that). And so are cats, he added (or something like that). But he couldn't think clearly. He couldn't talk and he felt woozy and giddy, as if he'd been anesthetized or hypnotized, and his feet no longer touched the ground.

They reached the gate. And, on the subject of cats, there was one sitting there. It was the Egyptian cat. Hyena sat down opposite her, and Dog followed suit, at which point the Egyptian winked very clearly, nodded toward a corner of the cemetery, and walked off with her tail held high, which is what all cats do at mealtimes.

"Let's follow her," said Hyena. "The Italian has just invited us to supper."

The Italian, the Artist, and the Egyptian

The Italian was the boss in the cemetery. Hyena had known him for ages. They were old friends. He was called the Italian because he'd been the favorite cat of a rich and refined old Italian actor, who'd fed his cats on salmon, pheasant, and real caviar. "It's outrageous," the actor's neighbors used to whisper, "when you think of all the starving people in the world!" But the actor's door was open to everybody, while his neighbors' doors were covered in locks.

The Italian used to live in the actor's home, with his three friends the Egyptian, the Artist, and Pinkie. The Artist was the sleek black cat who'd just been decorating the pink porphyry grave. It was Pinkie's grave. Pinkie was a fine, fat old dog, who'd spent eighteen years sharing the actor's home. Her long life had left Pinkie short of breath. Each day she used to climb the stairs more slowly with her tongue hanging farther out. She could barely breathe. And then one morning, when the Italian (the cat) woke up and went purring over to rub himself against her, Pinkie didn't flick her tail or wrinkle her nose, or even open an eye. She'd stopped breathing altogether because it had become too difficult.

There was no end to the actor's tears. "Crying his heart out for a stupid animal!" sneered the neighbors, who were callously waiting for an inheritance from their dead grandmother.

Pinkie needed burying. So the actor had ordered a gravestone of pink porphyry with gray flecks, exactly the same shade as Pinkie's fur, to be made for her.

From that time on the Italian, the Egyptian, and the Artist started mounting guard in the dogs' cemetery. It soon caught on and other cats joined them. Once in a lifetime a cat meets a dog who makes a lasting impression. Cats don't like dogs as a rule, but there's always one exception. And Pinkie was that exception.

The Egyptian, the Artist, and the Italian had taken over a disused kennel at the far end of the cemetery up against the caretaker's house. As soon as the Egyptian meowed (or was it cooed?) to announce Dog and Hyena's arrival, the Italian stepped outside to welcome them. He was a distinguished-looking black and white cat who was twice Dog's size. He appeared to be wearing a morning coat or a smoking jacket, with a white shirt front and a ruff of black fur like a bow tie. He seemed fun, gentle, and smiley, and his slow gestures showed that he took his hospitality very seriously. He stood in front of Hyena and Dog with a discreetly welcoming smile on his lips. Hyena raised his front leg as a sign of friendship and placed it on the Italian's shoulder. The Italian arched his back and came to rub himself against Hyena's chest. Then he looked at Dog, who was petrified and clumsily lifted a leg, thinking it would never reach the Italian's shoulder. But the Italian slid under Dog's paw with surprising agility, and rubbed himself against *his* chest too. For a moment Dog felt very tall and immensely proud of himself.

They went through the same ritual with the Artist. His fur was so perfectly black and shiny, it reflected the rays of light all the way from the bridge. These moving reflections were disturbing and beautiful at the same time.

Once everybody had been introduced, they went inside the kennel. The Artist had decorated it in exquisite taste with feathers, hangings, flowers, and furs from who knows where. In the middle of all this grandeur was the pheasant that Hyena had stolen: plucked, expertly carved, and ready to be eaten.

They ate in silence, as a sign of their appreciation. (The meal had been prepared by the Egyptian, and her sand-colored body was now stretched out on the fur rugs.) Not that Dog would have been able to say anything anyway. He was still reeling, and he felt as if he was floating higher and higher somewhere above the real world. But when the time came for them to go their separate ways (the lights on the bridge had gone out and the sun was rising), they had to say *something*: thank their hosts or pay them a compliment. It didn't really matter what as long as it was polite.

So Dog turned to Hyena and stammered, "Tell them we had a *really* . . . *really* . . . good time. . . . It was . . . it was . . . like a dream!"

His words prompted a strange flicker in Hyena's eyes, like an icy flash of anger (or something like that). Hyena stared at the Italian, and Dog saw the same disturbing flicker in the cat's eyes.

Have I said something wrong? wondered Dog.

But before he could find an answer, he heard a sharp clicking noise. A long claw shot out of the Italian's paw (just one, but what a claw!) followed by a hissing sound, and Dog felt a terrible burning sensation ripping his cheek.

Hyena didn't catch up with Dog until they reached the other side of the bridge.

"What did I do? What did I say?" whimpered Dog, who was still trembling all over from the shock. "Why did he scratch me?" He wiped his paw over his bleeding cheek.

"I told him to," Hyena answered.

"You *what*? Why did you ask him to do a thing like that?"

"To make you understand it wasn't a dream," replied Hyena.

And off he went, cool as a cucumber.

It took only a few days for Dog's wound to heal over. The scar formed a sort of grayish ridge where the fur would never grow back. Each time he felt the gash on his cheek Dog knew that just because he was happy, it didn't mean he was dreaming. And he began to enjoy living with Hyena and Wild Boar, without any worries or nightmares for company. He could have gone on like that for the rest of his life. But it didn't last. Dog left his two friends.

Why? That's a big question. Perhaps because, in Hyena's words, "The problem with life is that even when it seems the same, it's changing all the time."

Plum!

It was May. Spring was in full bloom. The days were getting longer. Dog was out walking by himself. He made a habit of it now that he knew the city almost as well as Hyena did. They would go off wherever the fancy took them, and in the evening they would tell each other stories about what they'd seen. But the business of mixed-up kids kept bothering Dog. So he started waiting at school gates. At about four in the afternoon he would sit on the sidewalk opposite and watch the children coming out. They burst into the street like a pressure cooker exploding, causing mayhem for the police, not to mention the drivers who had to slam on their brakes.

And then the inevitable happened. One afternoon Dog was sitting in front of a school, watching the children on the sidewalk opposite, when he heard an excessively high-pitched voice shouting his name.

"DOG! DOG!"

The traffic ground to a halt. The hair on the heads of passersby stood on end. Dog felt the blood in his veins flowing backward. There was no mistaking her voice; it was HER — it was Plum! She was standing by the school gate, her mouth like a big hole in the middle of all that red hair.

"DOG! COME HERE AT ONCE!"

Dog was frozen to the spot, and he didn't know what he really felt. Joy? Panic? The urge to jump into Plum's arms? The impulse to flee as quickly as possible? He didn't move. Nor did Plum. She clenched her fists and kept shouting louder and louder.

"I SAID COME HERE AT ONCE!"

The Earth must have stopped spinning. There was just a red-haired sun on the other side of the road, stamping its feet.

"DO I HAVE TO COME AND GET YOU?"

And she started crossing the road, dragging a backpack that was bigger than she was. The chaos that followed shook Dog from his daze: screeching brakes, blaring horns, whistles being blown, and all sorts of rude words being shouted.

She's not going to catch me — I'm gone!

By the time Plum had reached his side of the street, Dog was already ten yards ahead of her. He stopped to get a better look. She was the same, but different too. She was a bit taller, and her hair wasn't quite so straight; it was almost wavy. But her voice hadn't changed.

"ARE YOU COMING OR NOT?"

No! thought Dog, backing off another ten yards as she headed toward him. That enormous backpack was getting in her way, so she ditched it. Oddly this made Dog feel happy. The bag and its contents had always been his chief rival. Plum started running. He let her get close, almost close enough to touch him, and then he leaped up and ran to the end of the road. She stopped dead. She opened her mouth again, but this time no sound came out. So she closed it and kept walking, with pinched lips, clenched fists, and a determined look in her eyes. She was making slow progress. Dog waited for her without moving.

Two or three yards before reaching him, she stopped and took a look around. There was some construction equipment next to the sidewalk, where something was being repaired. Quick as a cat, Plum grabbed a stone and held it above her head. She aimed at Dog. Dog hesitated for a split second. Then, instead of running away or baring his teeth, he sat down with a bump, made himself look as idiotic as possible, and tilted his head to one side, with one ear drooping and the other pricked up. The effect was instant. Plum's hand opened automatically and the stone landed gently at her feet.

Her voice softened. "Please, Dog, *please* come here."

Dog almost gave in. Something melted inside him, a sudden wave of happiness washing over him. But instead of jumping to Plum, he leaped backward again. And when she began striding toward him, he set off too.

Dog led Plum a long way from school. At first she kept trying to launch surprise attacks. She'd walk along like a wide-eyed tourist and then all of a sudden she'd pounce. But Dog was keeping an eye on her. Plum's hands snapped at thin air. Dog was sitting in front of her again, out of reach. So Plum flew into a rage, shouting and threatening and stamping her feet. At other times she took some candy out of her pocket and crouched down with the bait, patient as a fisherman. Dog waited too. He waited for her to put away her silly treat. And then they were off again.

They were a very long way from the school by now. The evening was settling in. Plum had given up trying to catch Dog by surprise. "I'll just have to wear you out," was how Dog interpreted that steely look in her eyes. "You'll get tired before I do."

But that's not the way it turned out. Plum's legs were the ones that started feeling heavy. So she **134** switched tactics and started crying. She wept silently and looked at Dog as if he was the cruelest torturer in the world. Dog had never seen so many tears all at once. It was like a flood. Was he really that cruel? Was he a complete monster?

Dog was on the verge of throwing himself into Plum's arms, when a booming voice said, "Oh dear, little girl! What's the matter? What are you so upset about? Are you lost? Do you want me to help you find your way back home?" The voice belonged to an elderly man with a leather bag and shiny shoes.

"THERE'S NOTHING WRONG WITH THE LITTLE GIRL! SHE'S FINE! STOP STICKING

YOUR NOSE IN OTHER PEOPLE'S BUSINESS! CAN'T YOU SEE I'M BUSY? LEAVE ME ALONE OR I'LL CALL A POLICEMAN!"

"But . . . but . . ." stuttered the kind passerby. Then he skedaddled with his back against the wall.

Plum stayed exactly where she was, in the middle of the sidewalk, trembling with rage but angriest of all with herself. Dog realized what they had to do. They had to start all over again.

So they started all over again.

They walked along endless roads, crossed enormous squares, got muddled up in a maze of tiny streets, went down into underground passageways, and climbed steep stairways. On and on Dog and Plum went until it was completely dark outside. Plum didn't have any idea where they were anymore. Her feet were killing her, but she didn't care. All she could see was Dog. He was just a few paces ahead of her, a twinkle in his eye but as out of reach as ever.

As a last resort, she tried a different tactic.

"All right, Dog, you've won. If you don't want to follow me, go and do your own thing. Bye!"

She turned on her heel and walked away with purpose in her stride.

Dog watched her disappear around the corner. He stayed sitting. Three seconds went by, then ten and then fifteen, as he kept his eyes fixed on the corner of the building. When a minute had passed, the little head of red hair reappeared. But it wasn't the same sun as before — its fire had been put out. It was a pathetic little head, desperately wondering if Dog was still waiting. And yes, he was still waiting, sitting in the middle of the sidewalk with his head high. But what was he waiting for?

What's he waiting for? Plum wondered, frantically trying to find an answer. Dog was waiting for her to find that answer.

They stayed there for a long time, staring at each other like that. And then, just as they were both beginning to give up hope, the moment they'd been waiting for suddenly happened. Plum walked toward him. Dog didn't pull back. When Plum was level with him, she didn't try to grab him. And Dog didn't try to escape. Plum sat down on the pavement. Dog lowered his head and looked up at her.

At last Plum spoke. She said, "All right, Dog, I admit it. I was mean and selfish and stupid. I made you suffer and I abandoned you. It's all true. But what d'you want me to say? I want you to come back home. I miss you. I can't cry anymore because I've cried too much already, but I'm *really* sorry. Of course I can't make you come back. And it's no good telling you I won't behave like that anymore, because you won't believe me. But I really think . . . no, I'm positive I wouldn't treat you like that anymore. I love you too much. I've missed you too much. I won't do it anymore, I promise."

It came out in a very soft voice, almost a whisper, as she struggled to find the right words. She took off her shoes and then her socks. Her feet were in a sorry state.

So they decided to catch the subway home. They found the nearest station, then changed and changed and changed again, letting the cars cradle them (Plum was holding her shoes in her hands and Dog was rolled up in a ball on her lap) until they reached the station closest to the apartment. At last she was as calm and gentle as the Plum of the good old days. And Dog let out a sigh of victory.

Plum and Dog

So here we are back in the present again. Dog's been back with Plum for two months now. He's been back with Mr. Muscle and Mrs. Squeak for two months too, which is much less enjoyable.

When Plum turned up in the middle of the night, with her feet bleeding and Dog in her arms, Mr. Muscle and Mrs. Squeak had already alerted all the emergency services.

"Our daughter has disappeared! Our daughter has disappeared!" They were frantic. Mrs. Squeak thought Plum had been kidnapped. She was waiting, hand on the telephone receiver, for a ransom demand.

The neighbors were trying to reassure her.

"It might not be all *that* serious. Perhaps she was just run over by a bus!"

"Unless she's run away?"

"Or fallen in the river . . ."

They were doing their best.

Mr. Muscle was walking around and around like a bear with a sore head. He kept on saying, "If anyone's hurt her, if they've so much as touched a single hair on her head . . ." And he stared so fiercely at the neighbors, they had to look away. And then, all of a sudden, he broke down and wept. "My little princess, can't someone find my little princess?"

Suddenly, after midnight, the doorbell rang. Ding-dong! They rushed over to the door and opened it. There was Plum, barefoot, with Dog in her arms.

"Where on earth have you been? Aren't you ashamed of yourself? Do you have any idea what you've put us through? We've alerted all the emergency services! And what about the neighbors? What are the neighbors going to say? We're a laughingstock already. It's all because of that dog, isn't it? It's all that wretched dog's fault!"

They glared at Dog. They were even angrier than before, if that's possible.

And things haven't improved with time. In fact, if anything, they've been getting worse. But Dog doesn't care. Plum loves him, and her love is enough.

He's managed to complete the little girl's training in two months. His mistress is now his friend. He started off by teaching her that he was more important than her backpack, her dolls, her music collection, and her latest whim. Next, he refused to look sweet to impress her friends or to give her his paw in public. He taught her not to treat him like a performing dog in a circus, but as a real dog. He didn't mind giving her his paw; he didn't mind looking sweet just for her; he would even let her dress him up as a pop star. But not in public.

It's private! Between us!

He also showed her how to recognize a sick dog from a healthy one. If the tip of a dog's nose is dry and hot, it means he's sick. If the tip is cool and moist, it means he's healthy. Dog would make himself look as ill as possible, dragging his body as if there was no more blood left in his veins, and Plum would shout, "Dog! My God, you look so sick, Dog! Come here and let me make you better!" And she would busy herself

making him dishes of milk diluted with water, not for-
getting the yolk of an egg and some crushed eggshell.
"It's made of calcium and it's good for your teeth."

In short, Dog's managing it all rather well.

If Plum happens to fly into one of her famous
tantrums (which happens from time to time), Dog
turns his back on her, simple as that, and refuses to
look at her for days at a time until she's said she's
sorry. Which she eventually does. And, in return,
he's sensitive to her every need. He stops eating when
she stops, wipes away her tears when she cries, and
gives her parents such reproachful looks when they
scold her that they blush to the tips of their ears.
(Dogs are very good at doing this sort of thing.) He
walks her to school every morning and picks her up
every afternoon. He's an intelligent dog who knows
how to distinguish between a genuine desire and a
whim. He's also very loyal, while keeping his independence. He's left the apartment several times to go
and visit Hyena. ("You never ditch your friends. Not
for anything!") Hyena is always happy to see him.

"I'm staying with Plum," Dog tells him. "She's like
Wild Boar for me, you see."

"How did you manage to win her back?"

Dog grins from ear to ear. "I made her *want* me," he whispers.

"And her parents?" Hyena asks.

"They don't matter," says Dog.

"I'm not sure I agree with you there. You need to train them too if you want to live in peace."

Sometimes Dog spends two or three days out and about with Hyena. At first this put Plum in a sulk. And then she understood. He lets her play with *her* friends. They each have their own lives. That's the secret of friendship.

But her parents are a whole different ball game.

"He's such a tramp! Where's he been this time? Look how filthy he is! He's going to infest us with all the fleas in the city."

And Mrs. Squeak starts airing the apartment as if there's a dangerous gas leak. She polishes like a person possessed, running so fast behind the vacuum cleaner you'd think she was training for a marathon ("these wretched dog hairs get everywhere"), and cleans down to the last fraction of an inch. What a difference between this apartment and the happy shambles of Wild Boar's place! Nothing looks as if it'll ever move.

Thank goodness for Plum's room. Dog always hangs out in Plum's room. And Plum is always with Dog.

This is starting to annoy Mr. Muscle. "Can't your parents see you by yourself anymore? Does *he* always have to be with you?" And he gives Dog a foul look. "Gets on my nerves, that mutt."

Dog doesn't know it yet, but what Mr. Muscle is feeling is called jealousy. And jealousy is an extremely dangerous feeling.

Something Funny Goes On

Now we're back at the first chapter of our story. And the atmosphere is increasingly stifling. Plum's refusing to eat. And so is Dog. There's something funny going on. But Dog doesn't know what. For the first time in months his nightmares have come back. It's a bad sign. He woke up shouting, and Plum came looking for him. He fell asleep again in her bed. Now she's tucked up next to him, reading a Harry Potter adventure. Her favorite is *Harry Potter and the Goblet of Fire.* It's scary and funny at the same time: the perfect combination. Then she looks up from her book and strokes Dog, whispering, "My wizard." He lets out a contented sigh.

But the bedroom door opens and the day begins.

"What's that dog doing in your bed? We've told

you a hundred times: that dog is *not allowed* in your bed! We've had enough of this, Plum!"

"Enough of what?" asks Plum very quietly.

"All . . . this!" replies Mrs. Squeak, being deliberately vague. And she disappears.

A quarter of an hour later Plum and Dog appear for breakfast. Mrs. Squeak and Mr. Muscle break off their conversation awkwardly. Silence. All you can hear is the sound of butter being spread on toast.

And then Mrs. Squeak gives everyone a fright by shouting, "We're going on vacation tomorrow!"

Plum looks up. She stares hard at Mrs. Squeak. **145** There's a smear of hot chocolate at the corner of her mouth. "Where?" she asks, after a long pause.

"To the seaside, of course!" exclaims Mrs. Squeak.

Mr. Muscle doesn't say anything. Plum looks at him, then at Mrs. Squeak, and then at her toast. Before dunking it in her hot chocolate again, she asks, "Is Dog coming with us?"

There's a tiny pause.

"Of course he is!" Mrs. Squeak answers chirpily. How strange that she's suddenly in such a good mood. . . .

"Of course?" insists Plum.

"Of course," says Mr. Muscle. "We're hardly going to leave him here all alone, now are we? What kind of parents d'you think we are? Dog's coming with us, and that's all there is to it!"

Plum waits to see what the catch is. Here it comes. Mr. Muscle fiddles with his teaspoon and adds, "There's just one condition."

"Aha!" says Plum. But she doesn't ask what it is.

"He'll travel behind, in the trailer," announces Mr. Muscle after a silence. "That way, if he's ill . . ."

"All right," agrees Plum.

Mr. Muscle and Mrs. Squeak raise their eyebrows. They were expecting Plum to put up more of a fight.

Mr. Muscle gets up. It's his last day at work.

"I'll travel with him," declares Plum.

Mr. Muscle sits back down again. "Out of the question."

"Why?"

"It's illegal."

"So why should Dog do it?"

"Dogs are allowed to, but human beings aren't."

"Says who?" asks Plum, whose hot chocolate is getting cold.

"The highway code," answers Mr. Muscle, who's going to be late.

Dog follows the whole conversation very carefully. He knows they're deciding his fate.

Plum stands her ground. Mr. Muscle complains and points out how late it is. Plum won't budge. In the end Mr. Muscle gets up, takes the keys to the basement garage, and goes out. Plum's piece of toast quivers on the edge of her bowl, like a fish out of water. Mrs. Squeak has retreated to the kitchen, and the sounds of clattering dishes can soon be heard.

When Mr. Muscle reappears, he's carrying a large wooden box, which he puts down in the middle of the living room. "There you go!" he says. The box has a sliding door that opens and closes. It's a clever design.

"What about the holes?" asks Plum right away.

"What holes?"

"The holes for him to breathe through!"

"Goodness, completely forgot!" roars Mr. Muscle, going for his electric drill.

"And the window?" Plum asks, once the holes have been drilled. "You're not going to make him travel in the dark, I hope!"

"And a little window! But just one!" exclaims Mr. Muscle as brightly as a waiter in a restaurant, and he proceeds to grind away with his keyhole saw like a cartoon character in fast-forward mode.

Dog's kennel soon has a handsome porthole.

Plum walks around the kennel and thinks about things for a while with her chin in her hands. Finally she says, "All right."

Mr. Muscle grabs his raincoat and races off to work. He's at least an hour late.

And suddenly everyone feels more cheerful. Plum's hot chocolate has gone cold, so she gives it to Dog, who wags his tail and drinks it straight from the mug. Plum rushes into her bedroom and comes out again with all kinds of bits and pieces to make the kennel more comfortable. She spends the whole day working on it.

And while she's transforming the wooden box into a palace, Dog dreams about his vacation. He'll visit the town in the south again. He'll see the seagulls in the surf. He'll make a pilgrimage to the rubbish dump. He'll go and say hello to the lavender-smelling butcher. He might even take a peek inside the house of the blonde lady who mistook him for a rat.

His whole childhood . . . he'll be able to relive his whole childhood. He won't be going back to the dog pound, of course, but just being in the town will help him remember Woolly more clearly.

Through the Window

It's the next day. They've been traveling for hours. Dog can tell from all the bends in the road that they're not on the highway. He's right. Mr. Muscle had planned everything before setting out.

"We won't use the highway," he declared. "We'll take the back roads because they're more picturesque."

"Okay," agreed Plum, who didn't mind either way.

The trailer is swinging around and Dog is a little bit worried. But otherwise he's very comfortable. The kennel is spacious and prettily decorated, and his cushions are much softer than the back seat of the car. All things considered, he's better off in the trailer. He can't hear Mrs. Squeak squeaking or Mr. Muscle grumbling at his fellow drivers, which he must be doing by now. The only person he misses is Plum.

But as soon as they stop, the back door to the trailer opens, then the kennel door, and Plum appears, her hair all haywire and her cheeks flushed from the heat. And they hug as if they haven't seen each other for ten years. Then Dog goes off to cock his leg against a tree. After that he follows a trail of five or six country smells at the same time. He goes around in circles as if he is a puppy all over again. Grass! The sweet smell of grass!

But Plum calls him back. He's in her arms again, and back in the kennel as the trailer door closes once more. Off they go. They've gone through this routine two or three times since setting out. They must have left the city far behind now. They're right in the country where there are more bends in the road than anywhere else. It's a miracle Dog hasn't thrown up yet. The car always stops just in time. Thanks to Plum, Dog supposes. She knows him so well.

The car stops yet again. Everything's just the same as before. Except for the smells. They're still country smells, but there's now a faint whiff of the south too. We've completed more than half the journey, thinks Dog.

It's getting dark. They stop at a service station for gas, refreshments, and, in Mr. Muscle's case, a little exercise. (He touches his toes and then clasps his hands behind his head, swaying from side to side and panting like a seal. He finishes off by jumping up and down on the spot and punching the air.) There are a lot of trucks in the parking lot. They look like towering mountains of smoking, spitting metal. Mr. Muscle is in deep discussion with two or three truck drivers. Mrs. Squeak is dozing in the car. Plum and Dog are playing hide-and-seek in the bushes nearby. He always manages to find her, but sometimes he pretends he can't.

152

The horn toots and it's time to leave. (Mr. Muscle has a special horn with twelve notes, so there's no mistaking it.) Plum puts Dog back into his palace and closes the trailer door. The engine starts up, but all of a sudden the trailer door opens again and so does the kennel door. A pair of leather gloves throws a blanket over Dog. Someone grabs him before he can fight back. The trailer door is closed and Dog is horrified to hear the car pulling away. He finally manages to put up a struggle and tries shouting. But it's no use because his barking is muffled by the blanket. It must have happened quickly and silently, when the others were already back in the car.

Dog can't see a thing. The person carrying him has started running and climbs two or three metal steps. A door opens and then slams shut. Another engine revs up. It roars like thunder. In the middle of this racket, Dog can hear two men talking and laughing. He's being held down so hard, he can't even move. He's frightened of suffocating under the blanket. And those gloves remind him of another pair of leather gloves. A pair just like them: the men from the dog pound! Just thinking about it is enough to make his blood run cold. Dog is so frightened, he pees on the person who's carrying him. The man lets out a shout of anger and the driver bursts out laughing.

The next thing he knows, Dog is flying! Quite literally flying! He's been thrown out the window so roughly that the blanket unwinds itself. It's not until he's in midair that Dog opens his eyes. The first thing he sees is the ground rising up at a terrifying angle. He closes his eyes, bracing himself for the impact. He rolls to the bottom of a ravine, bouncing like the fridge. And then he faints.

On the Road

When he wakes up, it's blue night. And there's a full moon. Dog doesn't move at first. He's too scared he's broken something. And then he feels despair. Because all the evidence points to the fact that he's been abandoned on purpose, like thousands of other dogs over summer vacation. It was Mr. Muscle's idea. He must have asked those truck drivers to do his dirty work for him, and Mrs. Squeak must have agreed to it even though she pretended to be asleep in the car. They did it because they were jealous. No doubt about it — *that* was what they'd been cooking up for the past few days. And Plum didn't have a clue what was going on.

Plum! How will she react when she finds the kennel empty? And what will those two tell her?

Little by little, Dog feels something else growing inside him. It's different from sadness — it makes him think very fast and makes him feel hot. It's anger, real anger. As angry as a rabid dog, thinks Dog. And with his rage comes a ruthless desire for revenge. He feels ten times stronger than he used to. Without even realizing it, he's jumped to his feet. He's standing up and there are no broken bones. In three bounds he's climbed the ravine separating him from the road. The grass and bushes must have softened his fall. He's on the road now. It glows peacefully in the moonlight.

What should he do? Follow them or go back to the city? He considers the situation and makes a snap decision: the city. All he can think of is revenge. The plan comes to him in a flash. He's standing in the middle of the road with his nose at tarmac level, looking for something. What's he searching for? His own smell.

That's right, Mr. Muscle. D'you know *why* dogs cock their legs over *every* car tire they go past? To make sure they'll always be able to find their way back. That's what Hyena taught me. You're probably one of those fools who's amazed when an abandoned dog travels hundreds of miles to find his owner again. You idiot! No imagination, that's your problem!

These thoughts fly around inside Dog's head as he hunts down his *own* smell under the layers of other smells. He searches patiently. He knows he'll find it. And when he's found it . . .

When I find it, Mr. Muscle, believe me, I'll follow it right to the end. There are millions of smells as intricate as lacework spread all over the earth. They make up a dog's geography, Mr. Muscle, because we don't need maps or signposts, and we don't need to ask the way either. Once we're on the trail, we don't let go. Oh, and by the way, Mr. Muscle, I've just found my smell!

Hyena's Shadow

Eleven days later, at six o'clock in the morning, there's a scratching sound at Wild Boar's door. Hyena pricks up his ears. More scratching. Wild Boar wakes up and goes to open the door.

"It's you. You're in trouble, aren't you? Come in."

Dog enters. He goes straight to the kitchen, where he laps up two gallons of water and wolfs down the food in Hyena's dish. It takes him less than thirty seconds to tell his story to his friends.

I told you not to trust those two, thinks Hyena. But he keeps it to himself. There's no point rubbing Dog's nose in it.

"What are you going to do?" he asks.

Dog tells them his plan. It's simple but devastating.

Hyena has never seen Dog with such a look in his eyes. And he's never heard him speak so confidently either.

"When?" he asks quite simply.

"Right away!"

"No," Hyena replies. "First things first. We need to look after you, and you need to get some rest."

Dog pauses for a second. "You're right," he admits. "I need to get my strength back."

"Dog! Why don't you come in here?"

Wild Boar's calling him. He's run a bath. Dog isn't normally very fond of baths, but Wild Boar insists. "Stop making excuses. It'll do you good."

Sure enough, the hot water relaxes him, and so does Wild Boar's kind voice.

"Show me your paws. . . . Heavens above! That's some journey you've just made."

He lifts Dog out of the bathtub and rubs him down while telling him how brave and strong and loyal he's been. Wild Boar's voice is deep and low. And Dog is snuggled up against his chest, so it feels as if Wild Boar's talking *inside* him, which is very reassuring. It sounds a bit like Plum's voice when she comforted him outside the dog pound, or Black Nose's grunts when

Dog used to fall asleep snuggled against her. And on the subject of sleep, Dog's eyelids are growing heavy.

I mustn't fall asleep. I need to get going. But while he's thinking this, he notices a strange taste of hazelnuts in his mouth. He recognizes it straight away. It's the unforgettable taste of Black Nose's milk.

"There's no rush," whispers a familiar voice. "Just make sure you rest until you feel better. You'll need all the strength you can get for your plan."

"All right," answers Dog, "but stay with me while I'm sleeping."

"I'm here. Don't worry, you won't have any nightmares," whispers Black Nose.

"Good, I'll go to sleep then," replies Dog, who has, in fact, already been asleep for some time.

A Few Friends

The apartment is empty when Dog wakes up. There's a dish of meat and rice waiting for him in the kitchen. The dish is soon as clean as if it were new. Things are looking up. Dog can feel his strength returning. Time to get to work. He must have been asleep for at least two hours, if not three. There's not a second to be lost. And he can feel the anger rising up inside him again. The same anger he felt when he came to after fainting. The kind of anger that makes you think on your feet and makes you warm inside. That makes you feel as if no one can hurt you anymore.

So here he is, about to get his revenge. But just as Dog's about to go out, the door opens and Hyena appears.

"Well, well, well. . . . You've woken up?"

"Yes," answers Dog, "and I've got to get going. How long was I asleep for?"

"Two days."

"What?"

"Two days and two nights. It's now the morning of day three."

Oh, no, I don't believe it! thinks Dog. He does a quick calculation. Eleven days on the road plus two days asleep makes thirteen days. Plus at least a week to carry out my plan, by which time they'll be back. So my idea won't work.

"What's the matter?" asks Hyena after taking one look at his face.

"I've lost so much time," says Dog. "You should have woken me."

"Not on your life! You don't cross half the country without needing to catch up on some sleep."

"But you don't understand," answers Dog, getting annoyed. "I don't have enough time now to get everything done."

"Unless we help you," Hyena suggests gently.

"No. It's something I need to do by myself," says Dog, after a slight pause.

"What if you give us orders and we carry them out?"

"Who do you mean by *us*?" Dog asks, raising his eyebrows. "Who d'you mean by *we*?"

"A few friends," Hyena replies.

Which is a very vague answer. Hyena's "friends" means every animal in the city. It's also a very tempting answer, because if all Hyena's friends help Dog out, they'll get the job done in no time. And well done, too. But no . . . it'd never work.

"By the time we've got everyone together, it'll be too late." Dog is beginning to despair.

"Unless everyone's together *already*," says Hyena casually, heading for the kitchen. "You've eaten the whole thing?" he calls, pretending to be shocked. "Well, thanks a lot! Couldn't you have left me *something*?"

Dog follows, his tail between his legs, looking crestfallen. Hyena bursts out laughing.

"I was only joking. It was meant for you." He opens the cupboard with one push of his nose, rips open a bag of dry dog food, and begins chewing thoughtfully.

"Um . . . Hyena," asks Dog in a wobbly voice, "what exactly do you mean by 'unless everyone's together *already*'?"

"Sorry, what?" Hyena gives a little start. "Oh, yes, I'd completely forgotten. Would you mind opening the door?"

Dog opens the door to the apartment. He jumps backward. The Italian is sitting on the doormat, with his tail wrapped around his paws. The scar on Dog's cheek flares up again. The Italian doesn't turn a hair. He's very smartly dressed as usual, and his bow tie gleams against his white shirt front. The same discreet smile hovers on his lips, as if to say, "Hello, my dear, how are you?"

Making a considerable effort, Dog goes up to the Italian and holds out his paw as a sign of friendship. The Italian slides under Dog's paw and purrs as he rubs himself against Dog's chest. Then he goes back to the door and lets out a long meow that echoes all the way down the stairwell. The Egyptian appears next, then the Artist, and behind them at least thirty cats and dogs of every shade and shape and size. They're all Hyena's friends. Dog recognizes quite a few of them, including Fakir, the German sheepdog who lives in the cigar shop next door. It drives Fakir crazy having to sort out the thieves from the customers. "I'm hopeless when it comes to remembering faces. And I never know which person I'm supposed to bite. So I end up not biting anyone at all."

The animals just keep piling into the apartment. A lot of them are pets who, like Dog, have been abandoned over summer vacation. Once they've helped take care of Mr. Muscle and Mrs. Squeak, they have *their* owners to deal with.

"Are we ready?" asks Hyena.

"Let's go," says Dog.

The Break-In

It's the middle of the afternoon, and the animals are walking through the city. The streets are deserted in the summer. The animals look as innocent as the day they were born. You'd think the city belonged to them (as well as to a few burglars who are planning to take their vacations later). A childhood friend of Hyena's called Buster, who's muscular as a boxer, is carrying an enormous bundle without showing any signs of strain. The Artist is trotting along beside him. Or not so much trotting as gliding like a small black panther.

The Egyptian and the Italian are at the front, between Dog and Hyena. The whole procession makes as little noise as a falcon circling above its prey.

"Here we are," says Dog.

Hyena looks quizzically at the building where Mr. Muscle and Mrs. Squeak live.

"Very fancy. And spanking new. A handsome building, wouldn't you say, Mr. Italian?"

The Italian smirks.

The Egyptian goes into the courtyard alone, head and tail held high, as if she is a regular visitor. She reappears in no time, winks, and gives the all clear. Two cats have already climbed trees, taking up positions as sentries, and an old mastiff with a strong bark is sprawled by the door to the building. The rest go into the courtyard. Dog leads the way, jumping up onto the shed and then onto the caretaker's roof. (The caretaker is watching an incredibly noisy war movie on television.)

"Buster!" Hyena calls.

Buster drops his bundle and joins them on the roof in two bounds.

"Can you take care of that?" asks Hyena, nodding toward the kitchen window.

The window is closed, but not locked. "It's too small for a burglar," Mr. Muscle had said.

Buster lowers his head and flattens his ears. He hits the window with his small round head, and the glass shatters.

"I could have forced the door too," says Buster, a bit disappointed.

"It's a security door," Dog points out.

"So what?"

The Bombing of Pearl Harbor

The apartment is silent and empty. It's so clean and tidy, all the animals talk in hushed voices. They move on the tips of their paws from the kitchen into the living room. They take in the polished table, the dust covers on the armchairs and sofa, the new television in the corner, and the antique dresser that shows off the crockery instead of storing it. The bookshelves are bursting with encyclopedias (bought from door-to-door salesmen) whose pages have never been opened. The ashtrays have never had ash in them. None of the knickknacks has ever been moved, and a real fire has never been lit in the fake fireplace. The shutters allow in just enough light to create a religious gloom. The animals' paws sink deep into the carpet that Mrs. Squeak cleaned and shampooed before she left.

The satin bedspread in Mr. Muscle and Mrs. Squeak's bedroom glows like the sky at dawn and matches the salmon-colored lace curtains, fine as a wedding veil. Mr. Muscle's dumbbells and chest-expanders are in a pile next to the linen closet, which Mrs. Squeak has carefully locked. The bathroom is so clean you can see yourself reflected everywhere: in the mirrors and tiles, in the enamel of the bathtub and the gleaming panels of the washing machine, in the gloss paint on the wall. It makes you dizzy. It's like walking into an empty space and finding you're surrounded by a crowd of faces all looking like you.

Plum's bedroom is different from the other rooms. It's almost empty. The cushions, curtains, and bedspread have all vanished. And so has the rug that Plum used to put her feet on when she woke up in the morning. Despite Mrs. Squeak's protests, everything was used to decorate Dog's kennel. Dog's heart is clenched now, and he's more angry and determined than ever.

They meet again in the living room. All eyes are on Dog.

"So," says Hyena, "what shall we start with?"

Dog looks around. He hesitates.

"That?" suggests Hyena. And he carelessly knocks a mock-crystal ashtray into the grate and onto a block of fake marble around the fireplace. The ashtray shatters into a hundred pieces.

It's the signal they've all been waiting for.

The Italian lifts his paw. That single claw shoots out. In a flash ten cats are clinging to the top of the curtains. They slide back down using all their body weight to rip the material into shreds as they go. Once the curtains are in tatters, the cats attack the armchair dust covers.

"Watch out, everybody!" warn Buster and Fakir. Having forced their noses between the dresser and the wall, they're busy making a gap. They repeat their warning once they've disappeared behind the furniture. "Watch out, everybody. Stand back!"

The dresser teeters forward, then falls back on all four feet, teeters again, and finally comes crashing down onto the table, which promptly collapses under its weight.

"That's no way to do it!" complains Hyena. "It's much more fun smashing the plates one by one!"

"You want plates? Follow me into the kitchen," Dog invites him in a friendly tone.

Hyena's right. It certainly is more fun. The kitchen has a tiled floor, and the plates make a very satisfying sound when they smash — so do the glasses. Next are Mr. Muscle's favorite bottles of wine, which he brought up from the cellar for safekeeping. A determined old poodle has managed to get the oven door open. He jumps up and down on it, paws together, until the hinge gives way. Buster does the same with the fridge door, pushing it with his head until the final splitting noise. The fumes from the spilled wine are making everyone feel very merry.

When they go back into the living room, it's snowing. The cats are emptying every last feather from the cushions. The Italian watches dreamily. Meanwhile the Egyptian is carefully flicking through *The Encyclopedia of Trees and Flowers*. She turns the pages by damping her paw with her tongue. Then, with the other paw, she rips the pages she's already read. She's been through several hundred already. Dog stops for a moment to admire the show. Buster is bashing the windows with his head, smashing them one by one. He works patiently, methodically, and cleanly. The cats are busy scratching Mr. Muscle's record collection.

Hyena nods discreetly in the direction of the television set. The Italian likes the idea. Hyena slides behind the set, cocks a leg, and slowly sprays the back of it. Then everyone sits down in front of it and the Italian presses the on switch. Great special effects: a multicolored star spreads across the screen, followed by the *phut!* of a small explosion, and then thick black smoke starts billowing out. (Down below, on the caretaker's television, the Japanese air force is bombing Pearl Harbor and causing nearly as much damage.) Thick soot covers the walls and gets into all the fluffy bits of the carpet. Everyone's coughing and rubbing their eyes, and they are all filthy. It's the perfect excuse for a communal bath, so Hyena fills the bathtub.

While everyone's kicking and splashing, Hyena, Buster, and Fakir load the washing machine. But they don't fill it with clothes. They fill it with knives, forks, shoes, knickknacks, jars of jam, and Mr. Muscle's dumbbells. And then they turn it on. It makes such a din that everyone hides in Mr. Muscle and Mrs. Squeak's bedroom. The satin bedspread isn't a very good towel, but the sheets and blankets are perfect.

Now to the closet, and the party becomes a fancy dress ball. There's a big scramble for the clothes that have been tipped out onto the floor. The Egyptian has dressed up in the lace curtains. She looks very glamorous. You can see the admiration in the Italian's eyes. He's managed to rescue a real bow tie from the wardrobe, which is now empty. But where's the Artist?

"Artist! Yoo-hoo! Artist!" calls Hyena.

Silence. They strain their ears. No answer.

"I think I know what he's up to."

Buster rushes into the hallway. Everyone follows him. At this point the washing machine explodes, in full spin-drying mode. Everyone falls flat on their bellies, their heads buried in their paws, as knives and forks go whistling past their heads. Some even end up wedged in the ceiling. In a final convulsion the machine vomits a sea of jam and spits out the dumbbells, which bounce against the bathtub, causing the enamel to crack into hundreds of little pieces.

Dog opens his eyes again. The first thing he sees is Hyena sitting in front of him with a knife sticking out of his chest.

"HYENA!" roars Dog.

"Yes?" replies Hyena.

"Th-there's a knife," stammers Dog. "There's a knife in your chest."

Hyena looks down at the knife, says, "Goodness me, so there is. . . ." and drops down dead.

"NOOOOOOOOOO!" roars Dog, throwing himself at Hyena.

But Hyena giggles and opens his front legs. The knife falls to the ground. It was just a joke. Very funny.

They're all sitting outside Plum's bedroom now.

"Hey! Artist!" calls Buster. "Are we allowed in?"

Silence.

"Can we come in and have a look?"

The Italian gently pushes the door with his paw. It opens. They all gasp in surprise and admiration. Plum's bedroom is the only room in the flat to have been spared, and it looks magnificent. There are bunches of flowers everywhere. A rainbow of flowers and peacock feathers, which makes the room glow.

"A little bit feline for my taste," comments Hyena, "but very pretty all the same."

The bed is covered in a turquoise cashmere blanket with Chinese silk cushions around the edge. Spread on the floor there's a sheepskin rug so thick a Chihuahua might get lost in it. It's a piece of the living room carpet that the Artist carefully cut out before the television exploded. The Artist's head and tail are protruding from this fleece. He's making a final inspection. His tail swishes irritably in the air. He isn't entirely satisfied. There's something annoying him. Suddenly he fixes on the bedside table. He's worked out what it is. He lands on the tiny piece of furniture in one silent leap, pushes two flower arrangements slightly farther apart, and climbs back down again. It's as if a curtain has been opened, and between the two vases a portrait appears.

"That's *me!*" exclaims Dog.

He's right. It's a portrait of Dog, fast asleep. But it's a very handsome version of Dog, as he would have been if nature hadn't botched the job. And it really does look like him.

"Wild Boar did it while you were sleeping," explains Hyena. "We thought it might look good in Plum's room."

They're all clambering on top of each other to get a better look. But nobody goes in because they don't want to dirty the bedroom.

Nothing to Do but Wait

Dog doesn't go into Plum's bedroom either. He lies down outside her door and waits.

What's he waiting for? For Mr. Muscle and Mrs. Squeak to come back. And to see Plum again, of course. His heart beats wildly just thinking about her. But he wants to see the faces of the other two when they clap eyes on his revenge. Mrs. Squeak will faint. Mr. Muscle might kill him. Too bad. At least he'll have done what he set out to do.

His friends have all gone. They had other apartments to see to. Dog offered to go with them, but everybody understood he wanted to stay here.

"There are plenty of us," said Hyena.

Buster emptied the remains of his bundle. "A few extra things," he said, leaving Dog with more decorations for Plum's bedroom.

Dog's alone in the vandalized apartment now. It smells of fire and soot and jam, and all sorts of nicer smells (dog and cat smells mixed together) that Mrs. Squeak's bound to hate. She'll think it's unhygienic and she'll faint a second time. At least Mr. Muscle won't be able to kill him twice. Once you're dead, you're dead. You change into a tree and nothing else can happen to you. But for the time being, Dog feels very much alive. He can't stop thinking about Plum. **177** He can't stop his heart pounding. Plum's bedroom seems to have fallen asleep. The scent of flowers floats above all the other smells. And Dog is waiting.

Poor Plum!

He's waited for three days. On the afternoon of day three a key turns in the front door lock. But nothing happens as Dog expected.

He's sitting in the middle of what used to be the living room, like Napoleon after a battle, when the sun's set and everything's been destroyed. The front door closes again. Mr. Muscle and Mrs. Squeak are about to walk in. Dog isn't frightened.

Mrs. Squeak comes in first. Dog stares at her proudly. But Mrs. Squeak doesn't see him. In fact, she doesn't see anything at all. She's not the same Mrs. Squeak. There isn't even the shadow of a reaction. She's pale as death. Her face shows the marks of unimaginable grief. Tears have carved great ravines on her cheeks. She sleepwalks over the crackling garbage underfoot and heads toward Plum's bedroom.

And then Mr. Muscle appears. Dog is really shocked. Is it the same man? For a start, he doesn't look like a lobster anymore. And he seems to have shrunk. His muscles have faded away. His face is alarmingly wrinkled, his lips are taut and white, and his eyes blaze feverishly. He doesn't notice his surroundings either. He's carrying an old blanket in his arms and heading toward Plum's bedroom.

And what about Plum? Where's Plum? Dog looks in the hall: empty. On the landing: empty. Down the stairs: empty.

PLUM? PLUM?

He rushes into the little girl's bedroom. Mr. Muscle has spread the blanket over Plum's bed. And Plum, who's been inside the blanket all along, is lying down on the bed with her eyes closed. She looks so tiny . . . teeny-weeny, and desperately thin, so thin you can almost see through her. Dog feels the way he did when he was next to Black Nose, after the white door had spun around in the sky and . . .

PLUM!

He jumps onto the bed, throws himself at Plum, and licks her and licks her and licks her . . .

Until she opens her eyes.

"Oh! It's you. . . ." she whispers in such a rasping voice, he can't believe his ears. He freezes, and strains every muscle to hear her. And this time he can hear, very clearly: "Hello, Dog! How's things?"

And then he doesn't hear anything else at all. Partly because Plum's arms are around him and partly because Mr. Muscle is shouting.

"LOOK! LOOK! SHE OPENED HER EYES! SHE MOVED! SHE SAID SOMETHING!"

And all of a sudden there's a great commotion. Mr. Muscle grabs Dog and squeezes him against his chest, just like the lavender-smelling butcher did, and covers him with kisses. Then Mrs. Squeak does the same. Then Mr. Muscle hugs him again. Until Plum finally announces, "Don't mind me — I'm *starving!*"

Dog spends the night in Plum's bedroom. She tells him everything. As soon as she saw the empty kennel, she went on a hunger strike. To begin with, they tried to deny it, pretending it was her fault, that she must have forgotten to close the kennel door and then the trailer door properly. But she stuck to her guns. And so did they. After a week they started getting worried.

"The thing is, they *do* love me, you see. And I love them back. But they have to learn to love you too."

They were so worried about Plum that they put "lost dog" ads in all the newspapers. "You're like a real bandit now, Dog. Everyone's seen your photo." But because the ads didn't do any good and Plum was still refusing to eat anything, they went back to the place where they'd asked the truck drivers to steal Dog. "I'm telling you, it was a real investigation, just like the ones on the TV." But they didn't find any clues and Plum continued to waste away. Her parents despaired of ever finding a solution.

"In the end they decided to come back home because I was so weak. They wanted to take me to the hospital. And that's it, Dog. Now you know everything."

She holds up Dog's portrait. She tilts her head. "Is that you? Very handsome! But let me tell you something, Dog. You're much more handsome in real life."

Then she looks around. "My bedroom's fantastic. It's never looked so cool. We'll sleep safe and sound in here together."

Here's to the Future!

Now it's time to head gently into the future. It won't take Plum long to get better. And Mr. Muscle and Mrs. Squeak will adopt Dog properly as the family pet. Mrs. Squeak's happy to do this because Dog saved Plum. And Mr. Muscle is ready to take his hat off to a dog who can transform the apartment into a wasteland all by himself! Mr. Muscle tells his friends the whole story.

"No kidding! Dog covered hundreds of miles. And when we got back home, you should have seen the state it was in — Pearl Harbor after the Japanese bombed it!"

All this happened not so long ago. And today Mr. Muscle is perfectly happy to wait twenty minutes in front of every tire.